The Girl at Jungle's Edge

Cent tried hard, but she couldn't help being a little jealous of the new captain's daughter, who was so slim and sophisticated and whom everyone admired so much. It was jealousy that made her taunt Elizabeth into making that fatal leap when she obviously didn't want to—the leap that brought Elizabeth crashing to the ground in a funny twisted position . . .

Cent learns from this dreadful experience and Elizabeth readily forgives her. The two girls quickly become fast friends, as they try to unravel the mystery of the strange bearded doctor who appeared, apparently from nowhere, at the time of the accident, and as suddenly disappeared again. Why was he hiding in the jungle? Who was the lovely little girl at Jungle's Edge? Could she be his daughter—and was he perhaps a deserter?

Together Cent and Elizabeth cut through the tangle of misunderstanding and half-forgotten events that has obscured the past, in an absorbing, fast-paced mystery for girls. Carol Wilde's illustrations point up the humor, the pathos, and the excitement of the plot.

The
Girl at
Jungle's
Edge

BY CORA CHENEY

illustrated by
Carol Wilde

ALFRED A. KNOPF

New York

*To Mary Oldnall and her garden
and the children in the reading circle,
this book is affectionately dedicated.*

L. C. Catalog card number: 62-14772

THIS IS A BORZOI BOOK,

PUBLISHED BY ALFRED A. KNOPF, INC.

Other Borzoi Books for Young People
by Cora Cheney

THE PEG-LEGGED PIRATE OF SULU
illustrated by Ezra Jack Keats

THE DOLL OF LILAC VALLEY
illustrated by Carol Beech

by Cora Cheney and Ben Partridge

RENDEZVOUS IN SINGAPORE
illustrated by Paul Galdone

CHINA SEA ROUNDUP
illustrated by H. Tom Hall

The Girl at Jungle's Edge

one

"Milicent, get up."

Mrs. Hawkes stuck her head in the door and spoke briskly in the direction of Milicent's coppery head.

"Yes'm," grunted Milicent, turning over to reach for the rest of her sleep.

"Right now," said her mother, hurrying away.

Milicent stretched her shoulders, pulled the sheet up to her ears, and plunged over the edge into another pool of deep sleep. She didn't hear Jemima and her friend Bets open the door and come into the room.

She didn't stir when Jemima began to make up the other twin bed, the one in which nine-year-old Jemima slept.

"Let's make her pop. Let's make her hair stand on end," said Jemima to Bets.

"Like a fire?" giggled Bets. "Same as last time?"

Jemima nodded.

Bets perched on the foot of Milicent's rattan bed. Jemima stood on her own bed.

"Now," she whispered.

With a pair of jungle screams Bets and Jemima leaped onto Milicent's bed. They scrambled across her, tore the sheet from her rounded body, and yelled in her ears.

Milicent sat up in bed and shrieked.

Mrs. Hawes came running down the hall.

"It's all right, Mother," cried Jemima. "We just broke off her sleep, not her arm."

"You could have broken my *back!*" shouted Milicent, her face red, her freckles sticking out like luminous polka dots, her red hair standing up like a flame. "Mother, you ought to kill them. When I was their age—"

"But mother told you to get up," protested Jemima between giggles, as she and Bets hung onto each other in delight. "She told you—"

"Bets and Jemima, run along. I'll deal with you later," scolded Mrs. Hawes. "Milicent, come have your breakfast. I have big news for you."

Milicent struggled out of bed and slipped on her white shorts and blue jersey. The idea of having to share a room with that juvenile delinquent! It was the one drawback to living here on the Naval Base in the Philippines. Anyone who is fourteen needs privacy.

She slapped water on her face. The water was always lukewarm here. She felt sticky and jumpy. It was going to rain soon for sure. They were on the edge of the rainy season now, only a few more days of the constant sunshine, the sweet-smelling evenings, and the cool deep shadows on the jungle's edge.

Celie, the Filipina maid, padded barefoot into the dining room after Cent.

"Everyone else has eaten," said Celie. "Your mother said to give you papaya for breakfast and this Melba toast."

"What did the rest have? Chocolate pie?" asked Cent bitterly, looking down at her plump figure.

"No, just coffeecake and coconut honey and bacon and eggs," said Celie cheerfully.

"What do you eat, Celie?" asked Milicent, looking at Celie's delicate waist, her tiny figure.

"Mostly rice, some bananas, fish," said Celie. "But, Cent, I wish I could be round like you."

"You make me feel good, Celie. I think I live under a curse. Everything I eat makes me fat. If I didn't exercise I'd be a real tub, I'm so short. Where's Mother?"

"She's next door," said Celie. "She's getting people lined up to go meet the new Captain. He's coming today."

"Today? He's early. So that's the news. Has she found out if he has any children?" asked Cent.

"Yes, yes, yes," said Mrs. Hawes, who was coming in the door. "They are flying in a day early. The dispatch says he has one daughter, aged fourteen. But that's wrong. Someone said he had only been married a few years. Probably means a four-year-old girl."

"But I wish it were fourteen. Then there might be someone to take Tammy's place," said Cent sadly. How she missed Tam, her best friend who had moved back to California three weeks ago.

"Oh, you'll find another friend," said Mrs. Hawes.

"No, I'm glad the girl is only four," said Cent reflectively. "Captain Ellis is going to be Dad's commanding officer. If he had a fourteen-year-old daughter she might be impossible and I'd have to be her best friend just because Dad is Exec."

"Now, Cent, you know that's not true," said Mrs. Hawes.

Cent raised her eyebrows. "Anyhow, I'm glad she's only four."

"Cent, do you remember that song 'Welcome, Baby' that you Mariners sang on Scout Day? I wish you would get the Mariners together to meet the new family and sing that when they get off the plane."

"Oh, Mother," groaned Cent. "There isn't time to get everyone together."

"You only need a few," said her mother.

"It might be fun at that," said Cent, taking another bite of papaya. "We could all wear our uniforms. Maybe they'll even take our pictures for the station paper."

"I knew I could depend on you," said Mrs. Hawes. "Now I've got to run down to the Captain's quarters and put fresh flowers around and be sure the hospitality committee got the food in and the beds made."

"I wish we lived in those quarters," said Milicent. "They're so old and big and mysterious looking."

"Those quarters used to be the old hospital, back before World War Two," said Mrs. Hawes.

"Someone told me the hospital was bombed. Is that true?" asked Cent.

"I think so, but it wasn't entirely demolished. Just a wing of it. That original building dates back to ancient Spanish days. That's why the walls are so thick and the ceilings so high. But I can't sit here chatting. You get the girls together and come on the bus out to the airstrip by three o'clock at the latest."

"Aye, aye, Mother. We'll be there."

two

Milicent stood on the corner with Molly, Jessie, and Nancy, all in their crisp blue Mariner uniforms. It was hot, hot.

"Hurry up, Bebe," they shouted. The station bus was puffing around the corner, slowing down for the stop. Bebe came charging from her quarters, shoestrings flapping, scarf and hat in hand.

"Whew," she whistled as she fell into her seat. "I thought I'd never get off the telephone. Mary called to tell me she knew some interesting things about the new Captain. Then she wouldn't tell me what."

"I bet she just made that up," said Cent. "You know how Mary likes to tease."

Bebe looked around. "Only five of us? Golly, we'll have to sing loud."

"Everybody I called was going to Teen Club or swimming. Nobody cared about meeting a little four-year-old girl. Anyhow, in our uniforms we can make some kind of impression," said Cent.

At the airstrip the girls found a crowd assembled. It wasn't every day that a new commanding officer came. Cent's mother and two other ladies held leis of frangipani and sampagita. The photographer from the paper was there with his camera. The firemen's band, in new blue and gold uniforms, stood by, ready to break into "Anchors Aweigh."

There was a group of officers and men, Filipino workers, and a few families milling about in front of the airport building. Cent spotted Jemima darting in and out of the crowd, holding a lollipop lei for the new little girl. Several people carried WELCOME ABOARD signs held high on sticks.

Cent waved to her father who was standing by the gate. He had been acting as commanding officer in the last few weeks.

"Let's go stand near my father," said Cent. "If we stand in a straight line, not too close together, we'll look like a bigger group. Then when I say 'one two three salute,' snap to attention and begin to sing."

"Aye, aye, ma'am," giggled Bebe. "Suppose I muff?"

"What's so funny?" demanded Molly. "She's commodore, isn't she?"

"There it comes," someone called out. Far, far, up in the sky a tiny moving spot of black loomed and zoomed, closer and closer. There was a stirring and rustling among the people. The men stood straighter, and the ladies patted their hair.

"Square your hat, Bebe," ordered Cent.

The plane circled lower and lower, spiralling down. Commander Hawes glanced nervously at his watch and motioned to the photographer.

The plane nosed down to the runway. Bump, bump. The pilot braked the plane, taxied by, turned, and stopped it smartly and squarely before the gate. The noisy engines idled to silence.

The ground crew pushed the staircase out. Commander Hawes, followed by the committee with the leis, came out behind them. The door of the plane opened. With a smile and a handwave the new Captain stepped out as the band began to play.

"One, two, three—" began Cent. She stopped with a little gasp. Behind the new Captain came his wife, and stepping out of the cabin behind her came a beautiful girl, blond and slim.

Gold, almost platinum, hair hung to her shoulders. She

wore a trim blue suit, immaculate white gloves, and she stood poised in the doorway for a second, balancing herself on slender high heels. She was at least fourteen.

"Ow, ow, will you look!" hissed Bebe. "What a be-au-tiful doll."

"Uh, one, two, three, salute—don't sing," ordered Cent, her face flushing.

The Mariners snapped smartly to attention.

"Oh, I say, Mummy, Girl Guides, see?" cried the girl. Her clear precise voice rang out over a momentary hush.

Bebe snickered.

"At ease," ordered Cent.

The group was coming through the gate now. The welcome committee had draped the leis about the newcomers' necks. Mrs. Hawes signalled something to Milicent, who stood there with her face red and her mouth slightly ajar. The cool, shining girl came forward and held out her hand in an eager, friendly manner.

Milicent took her in with a penetrating glance. The girl was tall, but she carried herself gracefully on her high heels. Milicent looked down at her own fraying sneakers and suddenly felt clumsy and lumpy in her simple blue uniform.

"Hello," she said belligerently.

But the new girl didn't seem to notice Cent's awkwardness. "I'm Elizabeth Carson—that is, I mean I'm Elizabeth Ellis," she said.

Cent remembered her manners. "I'm Milicent Hawes and this is Jessie Jones, and Nancy Walters, and Bebe Mineli, and Molly Bryan."

"How was the trip, dear?" asked Mrs. Hawes.

"Rather tiresome. Oh, my ears!" She put her white-gloved hands to her ears.

There was a little silence. "The Mariners are all so happy to have you here. I know they'll want you to join," said Mrs. Hawes, glancing at Cent.

"Oh, yes, yes, welcome aboard," said Cent. At once the girls began to chatter little remarks of welcome. In a moment Commander Hawes came over.

"Elizabeth's parents want her to come with them in the staff car. You girls will have to visit later," he said.

"Certainly," said Elizabeth, turning away with him. "Do please come to see me. I have some wizard records."

The Mariners stared numbly at the back of Elizabeth Ellis. "Well," said Bebe, "great new things are in store."

"Hi, kids." It was Mary Hamilton motioning to them. "Want a ride home? Mother brought me out in the car at the last minute."

The Mariners crowded into the back of the Hamiltons' station wagon.

"Oh, I wish you could have seen your faces, you lovely creatures," teased Mary. "I was watching you. I'm glad I didn't warn you. I found out about her this morning."

"Well, gee, thanks," said Jessie scornfully. "It was good of you to cut us in. Where did she pick up that funny speech?"

"Oh, don't be mad, Jessie," laughed Mary. "I thought it was so cute of you to plan to sing 'Welcome, Baby' to that glamour girl."

"How did you know about her?" asked Cent. "Even my father was surprised." She squeezed herself farther into the corner.

"Because I had a letter this morning from a girl I used to know in Newport. She said she had met an English girl who was coming out to the Philippines and that her stepfather was going to be commanding officer of the station. She told me she was a gorgeous girl, and that she would probably take over."

"English? How come?" asked Jessie.

"Take over? Who says?" asked Milicent with an unexpected edge to her voice.

"That's all I know about it," said Mary. "I guess you'll have to ask her yourself."

three

Cent thanked Mrs. Hamilton for the ride and got out in front of her quarters. She declined Molly's insistent invitation to go swimming. She felt a heaviness, a mood of depression, a foreboding about this new girl. How she missed Tam. She wanted to throw herself across her bed and think about it alone.

But she didn't have a chance. Celie met her at the door.

"Your mother just telephoned," she said. "She wants you to get dressed, dressed up, she said, and be ready to go out to dinner at the Officers' Club. Your father is taking the new Captain's family out to dinner, and they want you to entertain the new girl."

"I don't see why I can't go," pouted Jemima, who was already home. "I never get to go anywhere."

"Where did you get that candy?" asked Cent. Jemima was lolling on the couch sucking a lollipop.

"That girl was too old for the candy lei so Mother let me have it," Jemima said with a loud smack. Cent shuddered.

Another time I'd love going out to dinner with Mother and Dad, Cent thought, and without that revolting Jemima along.

"What's the matter, Cent, you jealous of that new girl?" asked Jemima, giving a slurping lick to her candy.

"Certainly not," snapped Cent. "And stop making those awful noises."

"She's pretty," said Jemima, giving another smack. "And I'm going to have chocolate pie for supper, and Bets is going to eat with me, and we're going to eat the whole pie."

"I hope it makes you sick," said Cent, and she slammed off to her bedroom.

"What's the matter with Cent?" asked Celie. "She gets mad sometimes but never cross like this."

"Oh, I don't know," said Jemima, wiping her mouth on her shirttail. "Mother says Cent is at a difficult age. Anyhow, she's not any fun any more. She thinks everybody is looking at her all the time. She thinks everything she does is so darned important. She's just nuts I think, her and all her nutty friends."

Cent stripped off her Mariner uniform and tossed it in a heap by the door. Standing in the center of her room in her bare feet and her brief undies she looked at herself in the long door mirror.

"I'm shaped like one of those egg timers," she muttered.

She flung open the closet door to push the mirror from her. Her simple wardrobe hung there before her. The dresses were all cool cottons, made alike on childish lines. At the other end of the closet hung Jemima's dresses, many of them exactly like Cent's.

On the floor below stood Cent's only pair of good shoes, flat-heeled white pumps. Cent pulled a pink checked seersucker dress from the rack, then put it back. The solid blue piqué had a rip in the side. Mother had told her to mend it, but it hadn't seemed worth while before. Too late now.

The green flowered dress was possible. Cent had not worn it much. It looks like an old lady's dress, she had thought when the box came. Grandmother had sent it to her for her birthday. Cent held it up to herself and pulled the mirror door around. The shades of green leaves and flowers on the white backgound made green shadows around her eyes.

But those shoes. Cent remembered Elizabeth's two-inch heels and stared unhappily at her run over flats.

"Why don't you try on Mother's straw pumps?" asked Jemima.

Cent jumped. Jemima was peeping through a tiny opening in the door. Cent shoved down her impulse to snap at Jemima.

"Maybe I will," she said tentatively. "Go get them. I think they'd fit if Mother will let me wear them."

"I've got them here," said Jemima. "I've been watching. Here come Mother and Dad, and you aren't nearly ready."

"Thanks, Jemima," said Cent. She slipped on the shoes. "Here, how do they look?"

"Cool," said Jemima. "Real cool."

Still in her underwear, Cent stood in the center of the room and looked at her feet. The shoes fit perfectly. Cent teetered a moment, regained her balance. The heels made her feel inches taller.

She took a tall breath and pulled herself up as far as she could. She took a few tentative steps on the shoes. Why, it was no trick at all.

"Look, Mother. Look how tall Cent is," called Jemima.

"Oh, Mother," Cent flushed slightly at her mother's quizzical expression, "I don't suppose you'd let me wear them, would you?"

"I don't see why not," said Mrs. Hawes thoughtfully. "I have another pair I can wear. Why yes, I think they'll be lovely on you, Cent. My, you're growing up."

Cent, bathed and powdered, slipped the green dress over head, put her feet into her mother's shoes, and sat down at

her dressing table. Carefully she combed her hair. She patted a tiny bit of powder on her nose, touched her lips with an orange lipstick, and then after staring at herself for a moment she tentatively put a tiny bit of cold cream on her eyelids. She batted her eyes at her reflection a few times and stood up. A satisfactory warmth came over her. She looked nice.

She probed her mind for a moment and took a furtive look at a little coil of jealousy that lay in her heart.

"Come on, Cent," called her mother.

"Coming, Mother," she answered without moving. She looked again at her reflection. Suddenly she ran her hand through her hair, messing it up with a characteristic gesture.

"I hate myself," she told her reflection. "I'm going to be nice to that girl if it kills me. Or her."

four

"Aren't you dying to know about Elizabeth's British accent?" asked Mrs. Hawes as they started out in the car.

"Mary gave me a clue," said Cent, glancing at her shoes, "but tell me anyhow."

"Captain Ellis was a bachelor stationed in London. He met Elizabeth's mother, a widow, and they were married a year ago."

"How long did they live in the States?" asked Cent.

"Not long, I suppose. Elizabeth was in an English boarding school until recently."

Commander Hawes drew up to the front of the Captain's quarters. The house was old and dark with heavy bougainvillea and other tropical vines pushing at the corners. Large-leafed trees shaded the driveway and the front door.

Elizabeth, wearing a blue-striped cotton and the same high-heeled shoes, waited by the door with her parents.

"Oh, this will be wizard," she exclaimed as they drove away to the club.

"It's okay," said Cent laconically. She fought back the hard little knot inside herself. "Your dress is pretty, Elizabeth," she said.

"American clothes feel wonderful after the dreary rags I wore in boarding school," said Elizabeth.

Things might have gone well from there, Cent thought later, if only the terrible incident hadn't happened. Elizabeth got out of the car first. Milicent, self-conscious in her high heels, scrambled after her.

It was because of the scrambling, in the heels. Cent's second heel caught in the floor mat of the car. She turned, teetered, fell, sprawled out for all the world to see, flat on her face on the sidewalk under the marquee of the Officers Club.

And Elizabeth, as quick as wind, turned and helped her up. Commander Hawes, leaping from the car to rescue her, cried out, "Oh, Jane, I told you she's too young to manage those cursed high heels."

The evening was not a success.

Cent sat stonily at the table, paying attention to her lean roast beef and green salad and sherbet while from the corner of her eye she watched Elizabeth tuck away french fries, buttered lobster, and chocolate éclairs.

Elizabeth herself fell into a deflated silence. Twice Captain Ellis asked Elizabeth if she were sleepy.

"Not really," said Elizabeth looking away.

She never looks at her stepfather, thought Cent.

But immediately after dinner Captain Ellis said that they were all very tired and should go to bed early.

"I never want to see her again," said Cent tightly on the way home. "I hope she doesn't come to the Mariner meeting."

"It's nothing to brood about," said Commander Hawes stoutly. "You weren't hurt. You've had hundreds of worse falls. I still say those shoes—"

"Please, Chuck," said Jane Hawes. "Let's not talk about the shoes any more."

Cent felt a welling affection for her mother. For a mother who was sometimes so obtuse, she could be understanding.

"But, Milicent," said her mother briskly, "if Elizabeth comes to the Mariner meeting, you must be yourself again as though nothing had happened. She has been invited. Remember?"

The next afternoon Bebe brought Elizabeth to the Mariner meeting at the boathouse. I'll bet she doesn't know how to sail, thought Cent proudly recalling her own sailing citation.

All eleven of the Mariners were there.

"Isn't it wonderful? Elizabeth was a Girl Guide in England," said Nancy gaily.

"And she can sail too," cried Molly, looking at Elizabeth with admiration. "Too bad the boat is in dry dock."

"Oh, not really very well. I did have a try at it when Mummy and I went holidaying at Torquay," said Elizabeth modestly.

"Let's get on with the meeting," said Cent, with an unaccustomed air of grim business.

Bebe raised an eyebrow at Mary. "And she studied dancing with a teacher from Sadler's Wells," she said.

"We'll have the reading of the minutes. Except for a party this will be our last meeting of the summer," said Cent, ignoring Bebe. Sadler's Wells?

There was a scuffle and giggles in the direction of the secretary, Jessie.

"Hab'm gott'm," came Jessie's muffled voice.

"What do you mean, you haven't got them?" asked Cent testily.

There was wild laughter from Jessie's corner.

"She's got a caramel stuck in her braces," snickered Nancy.

"And she's got her old algebra notebook instead of the minute book," squealed Mary.

"Unngh," grunted Jessie. "Oops, now I can talk." She was hit with a fit of giggles but stopped at the sight of Cent's stormy face.

"I didn't mean to, honest, Cent. I just picked up this black notebook, and I thought it was the minute book. I didn't know it was going to be my old algebra notebook."

Everyone but Cent was convulsed with the idea of bringing an old algebra notebook for minutes. Elizabeth whooped with the rest.

"I move," said Molly, taking a look at Cent's face, "that we dispense with the reading of the minutes."

Mary seconded the motion, and the meeting jumped along on routine matters.

"I want to suggest a service project for the last meeting," said Bebe, waving her hand wildly. "Let's have a welcome aboard party for Elizabeth."

There was a stir of agreement, and Elizabeth ducked her head in pleased confusion.

"All right," said Cent. "Do you have any suggestions?"

"Let's have a dance and every girl invite three boys," said Mary.

"After the last one Mrs. Muller said we'd have to wait three months," reminded Cent.

"Mrs. Muller is our advisor," whispered Bebe to Elizabeth.

"How about a swimming party?" said Molly.

"Too tame, too tame, we'll be doing that anyhow," Nancy objected.

"Hey," shouted Bebe, "Ellen's got a good idea."

"It was just about the clothes for the Negritoes," Ellen said in her quiet voice. "You tell them, Bebe."

"No, you tell us, Ellen," said Cent. "Be still, everybody."

Ellen twisted her handkerchief.

"You remember Mrs. Muller suggested we might get some clothes together for the Negritoes. I-I did. I asked around our street, and I have a basket full of children's clothes for them. Molly got some too, and—"

"Good!" interrupted Cent. "The rest of us had better get on the ball. You see," she explained politely to Elizabeth, "the Negritoes are pygmies, aborigines, very little people. There is a tribe of them who live up in the jungle not far from here."

"Really?" said Elizabeth, looking interested. "In the jungle, you say?"

"Yes, they live in trees, some of them, or little grass huts."

"This sounds like a geography lesson, not a party," cried a voice from the corner.

"Go on, Ellen, tell us the rest," said Cent.

"My father says he'll get a truck and drive us all to Jungle's Edge and we can deliver the clothes ourselves and talk to the Negritoes."

"Good thought, Ellen," said Mary.

"And," continued Ellen shyly, "Mother would like to have us all come back to our quarters for a picnic supper. We could make it in honor of Elizabeth."

"Yowee!" cried Bebe, "I'll come. Yum, yum."

"Ellen's father is commissary chief," explained Molly to Elizabeth. "They'll probably have the best food you ever ate."

"Ripping," said Elizabeth.

"Dad says he can get the truck next Monday. We have to go soon before the rains come. We could meet here at two o'clock and bring the clothes."

"Monday it is then," said Cent. "Yes, Molly?"

"It's scary at Jungle's Edge," said Molly. "Maybe we ought to just send the clothes. Something might happen there."

Cent laughed. "Nothing's going to happen. See you Monday."

five

The next day Cent found herself with time on her hands. School had been out for two weeks now. Normally she would have been off doing vacation things with the girls, but not today. It wasn't, she told herself, that she was avoiding Elizabeth. She just wasn't going to seek her out.

And Elizabeth was bound to be where things were popping. She was that kind of a girl. Besides, Bebe and Mary would see to that. It was tough to have Tam go away just as vacation came.

Cent practiced her dancing alone in her room. At first, Mother had made her take ballet lessons to reduce. But now, Cent thought, glancing in the mirror, it was exciting to hold herself, move herself, with studied control.

Mrs. Hawes stuck her head in the door. "I'm glad you are practicing. Did you know that Elizabeth is quite a dancer too? Perhaps she might like to join your class."

Cent continued her practice and made no reply. If Mother would only stop trying so hard.

Elizabeth will be way ahead of me, thought Cent bitterly. I know it. She can do everything better. But she practiced until lunch time, and during siesta time she stayed in her room reading *Rebecca*.

She read throughout the afternoon and went to the pool after the crowd had left. The next morning she slept late, and then she read again into the afternoon. It was hot. Should she go to the pool now? Molly arrived just as she began another chapter.

"Oh, Cent," said Molly flopping down in the glider beside Milicent, "what's the matter with you? You haven't been at the pool for two days."

"I just didn't feel like it," said Cent. "You know I like to read."

"I know you always have your nose in a book," said Molly, "but you always manage to be around places too. You really ought to see that new girl swim. She has a white bathing suit and a cute cap that looks like a French sailor's hat, and everybody was looking at her. And gosh, she can swim and dive real well too."

"Wizard," muttered Cent under her breath.

"What did you say?" asked Molly.

"Nothing," said Cent. "But some other people can swim and dive too, Molly."

"Oh, sure they can," said Molly. "Of course I can't swim and dive as well as she can, but you can, Cent. Oh, nobody is better than you, even if some of the others say so."

"Well, thanks, Molly," Cent laughed. Nobody could be mad at Molly. "You're sweet, even if that was a left-handed compliment."

"A what?" Molly looked at Cent in a puzzled way.

"Skip it," said Cent affably. "I'll go to the pool with you if you really want me to."

"I'm glad," said Molly. "Some people are wondering why you aren't around so much any more."

Elizabeth had left when they got to the pool, so it was almost like old times. Cent practiced her jackknife dive and swam the pool eight laps.

Elizabeth herself telephoned on Monday morning.

"I say," she said, "I'm flummoxed by this clothing thing. Mummy told me to get through to you. You see, we haven't any old children's clothes. Only my own new things."

A small thing indeed, but Cent had a momentary sense of elation.

"Don't worry," said Cent. "I have plenty of Jemima's old things. I'll divide with you."

"How kind of you," said Elizabeth. "Thank you indeed. Cheerio."

"That child must be having an awful struggle," said Mrs. Hawes as she gathered up some of Jemima's outgrown clothes.

"What child? You mean the Negrito children?" asked Cent.

"Oh, they have a struggle too," said Mrs. Hawes. "Their struggle is to survive in the jungle. But I was speaking of Elizabeth Ellis. She has the problem of surviving in civilization."

"Her?" Cent sputtered, looking at her mother in amazement. "Sorry for her?"

"Of course; aren't you?" said Mrs. Hawes quizzically. "Or maybe it hadn't occurred to you that Elizabeth is operating under a terrible strain."

"It certainly hadn't occurred to me," said Cent with a touch of disdain. "What kind of a strain?"

"First of all she has a stepfather who is utterly strange to her. And she has a new name, and a new country, and a new mother."

"A new mother? Really, Mother, what are you talking about?"

"Suppose for a minute, Cent, that just you and I lived all alone together. Then a man, utterly strange to you, came to live with us and most of my attention was turned away from you to him. Don't you suppose it would make a change in me? The whole pattern changes. See? Relationships are utterly different."

"We-el, I see your point," said Milicent slowly. "But I can't see that Elizabeth has had it so tough. Boarding school, travel, and then to get to come here and live in those gorgeous quarters. Plus all her celebrated accomplishments."

Mrs. Hawes didn't answer immediately. She turned to Cent and handed her the clothes.

"I want you to look up a couple of words in the dictionary for me, Cent," said her mother lightly.

"What words?" Cent loved words.

"*Acrimony*," said her mother. "And *compassion*."

"Oh, those are easy," said Cent. "I already know those."

"But I want you to look them up anyhow," said Mrs. Hawes.

"I'll do it later," said Cent. "It's time to go now. I have to see that all the clothes are bundled up and that the girls have on the right kind of shoes. Mrs. Muller said we had to wear sturdy shoes today."

"You're a very dependable girl, Cent," said her mother. "And a good leader. But don't forget to look up those words. I'd like you to study their meanings carefully."

"Okay, Mother, but later. I promise that tomorrow I'll make a study of acrimony and compassion."

six

Chief Dean was at the boathouse with the truck when Cent arrived at ten minutes of two.

Several girls, lugging parcels of clothes, were coming down the street. Elizabeth was with them.

"Let me have the gear," said Chief Dean. "I'll put it in the truck."

"And the first-aid kit, too. I have the snake-bite kit in it. I'm always so afraid somebody is going to get bitten by a cobra," said Mrs. Muller, who had just arrived.

"Or squeezed to death by a python," cried Mary in a deep voice, running up behind Mrs. Muller and giving her a breath-taking squeeze.

"Oh, Mary," squealed Mrs. Muller. "You mustn't scare me so. I don't see how I have the nerve to be responsible for you crazy girls."

The girls piled into the back of the truck, and Mrs. Muller sat up front with Chief Dean.

The truck slowed down at the gate. Now they were off the navy base. Singing, laughing, swaying in the back of the open truck they bumped over the narrowing, winding, road that led to Jungle's Edge.

On either side the jungle surged down to the bare strip of rocky road. Once beyond the mountain road the country would flatten out into rich rice fields, but here in the mountains the growth was heavy and mysterious.

Caught in the immensity of the jungle the girls stopped singing. They looked up at the enormous mahogany trees with their strangling vines and at the dense underbrush below.

"Why is it called Jungle's Edge?" asked Elizabeth. "Is it a special place? I mean, isn't all of this the jungle's edge?"

"It's a special place," said Cent with a trace of superiority. "It's where the side road ends, a clearing. The Negritoes live there, or rather they live in the jungle around there. But if the people, us, or the town people, want to see the Negritoes they come to Jungle's Edge and the Negritoes will come out and talk, especially if we bring presents."

"But can they speak English?" persisted Elizabeth.

"Some of them can. They talk to each other in some odd dialect, but some of them have learned English. Once in a while the Negritoes will come to the Base with their headman, or king as they call him, and trade bows and arrows for cigarettes. The men on the ships love the bows and arrows for souvenirs."

"Sounds supersonic," said Elizabeth.

They had turned off the road now and were easing down a rough path. Ahead they could see a clearing. Chief Dean steered the truck over a deep rut and pulled it to a stop on the grassy bank.

Cent and several others started to stand up, ready to hop off the truck.

"Wait," cautioned the Chief, leaning his head out the window to make sure he could back around. "I like to be headed out when I stop my bus. You never know when you'll need to leave in a hurry."

"Oh, what could possibly happen to anybody here?" said Mary, glancing about her. "These little Negritoes are gentle as dolls."

"Well, you never know," said Chief Dean. "I'm going to back up now. No sense in taking any chances."

seven

When the truck was turned around and headed towards the main road Chief Dean stopped the motor. There was no sign of life anywhere.

"Wait a minute, girls," said Mrs. Muller. "I think we'd better let Chief Dean go first. Are you sure this is the place? I don't see anybody around."

"Don't worry," said Chief Dean. "I expect we're surrounded. The people are looking out of their houses now."

"What houses?" Mrs. Muller looked anxiously around her.

"Oh, I see some houses," said Milicent. "See? Over there in the grass."

The girls all looked. There was a cluster of tiny thatched huts, so much the color of brown grass that they could only be found by searching.

"Be careful where you put your feet. There might be snakes," said Chief Dean. "Let's all stay together and walk over towards the huts slowly. I've been here before. The headman knows me."

But before the last girl could clamber from the truck four little heads appeared not over six feet away. They were Negrito children, tiny, naked, laughing.

"Oh, aren't they sweet?" said Cent, pausing. The children ducked down into the grass and appeared again several feet farther on, still giggling shyly.

"Here comes the headman," said Chief Dean.

Approaching him was a small dark man not over four feet high, but his erect carriage made Cent forget that he was a pygmy. He was dressed in a loincloth and an old army shirt.

"Welcome," he said. "Will you come to my house?"

"Thank you," said Chief Dean. "The Mariner Scouts have brought you some clothes."

The headman's eyes glistened as he saw the bags of clothing. These things would keep his people covered while the cool rains fell.

"Smoke?" Chief Dean offered the man a cigarette. Solemnly the Negrito king took the entire package of cigarettes and tucked it into his belt.

The girls stood silently behind Chief Dean. Behind the Negrito leader gathered shy, tiny women with doll-sized babies on their backs, young men, old men, and children.

They were wild and strange looking, uncivilized, and half-naked, but their faces were friendly and trusting and their eyes eager.

Cent made a gesture forward, holding out her sack of clothes. A woman behind the headman held out her hand eagerly. Cent pulled a small shirt from the bag and held it up. There was a general movement, a surge forward, and in a moment the girls were mingling with the Negritoes.

There were little cries of admiration.

Chief Dean and the headman walked toward the most elaborate of the straw houses, talking.

"Wait," Chief Dean motioned to Cent, "ask the girls to bring all the bags of clothes to the headman's house. He will distribute them."

"That's a good idea," said Mrs. Muller. "The shyest ones will get nothing otherwise."

The girls put their offerings on the bamboo porch of the headman's crude little house. The Negrito children ran about like puppies, pointing and laughing. Suddenly they were playing a game of follow-the-leader, running and jumping through the grass.

The leader ran to the edge of the clearing where a giant tree dripped a strangling vine over the grass. He grabbed the end of the vine and swung Tarzan-like over the grassy gully and dropped off into the grass on the other side.

The vine flew back and the second child grabbed it and with a running start moved freely into a high arc. Then another and another and another.

"Come on," cried Bebe, "let's play too!"

"I'm a jungle girl," shouted Mary, running after her. At once, the whole troop of Mariners was running toward the jungle sky ride.

Elizabeth hung back a moment.

"Come on," cried Cent, pausing.

Still Elizabeth hesitated.

"What's the matter?" asked Cent scornfully. "Are you afraid?"

The other girls were ahead, ready to leap over the ravine, shouting with delight.

Elizabeth began to run along with Cent, following the other girls.

"Is this all right? Is it safe?" asked Mrs. Muller anxiously, turning to Chief Dean.

"I think so. The vine looks strong enough, and there's grass below."

"It will hold," said the headman in his stilted voice. "Even the men swing on it."

"I'll go have a look, just in case," said Chief Dean. He strode across the clearing. The cluster of laughing girls stood together waiting for the vine to swing back.

"Me first," cried Cent cockily. "If it'll hold me it'll hold anybody."

"Well said. Let Cent test it," shouted Bebe.

Cent grabbed at the swinging vine, gave a running start, and flew out in a wide arc over the ravine, landing safely on the other side.

"Elizabeth next," she cried as she fell into a relaxed heap on the soft grass.

Elizabeth hesitated, standing uncertainly before the swinging rope.

"Come on!" cried Cent.

Ellen, standing beside her, cried out, "Elizabeth, don't!"

"She's terrified. Stop her!" shouted Chief Dean.

But it was too late. Elizabeth tensely grasped the dangling vine. She leaped out, swinging above the ground, and flew through the air.

eight

Stiff and rigid, Elizabeth's slim body shot into the air. Ellen put her hands over her eyes. Cent, rising from the ground where she had remained comfortably relaxed, sensed rather than saw that something was wrong.

It could only have taken seconds. Momentum pulled Elizabeth into the zenith of the arc. Cent let out a scream as she saw Elizabeth's stiff arms suddenly relax. Elizabeth went hurtling to the ground.

Chief Dean leaped down the side of the ravine, followed by the Negrito king. Elizabeth lay white and gasping on the ground. "She must have fainted with fright in mid-air," he said.

Cent threw herself down the other bank.

"Oh, it's my fault! It's all my fault!" she cried hysterically. "I egged her on when I knew she was scared."

"Hush, hush, Milicent," said Mrs. Muller who ran up with the first-aid kit. Mrs. Muller's face was as white as Elizabeth's. Obviously Elizabeth was hurt far past the capacity of the first-aid kit.

"Get a blanket from the clothes. I brought one to give away," commanded Mrs. Muller.

Dazedly Cent ran to the hut for the blanket.

The Negrito king leaned over the injured girl. He barked a word over his shoulder. The other Negritoes who had crowded around moved back at his command. He uttered a few more words, and a young man from the group nodded knowingly and darted off into the forest.

Cent ran back with the blanket.

"Do nothing," warned the headman as Mrs. Muller and Chief Dean prepared to lift Elizabeth onto the blanket. "White doctor is coming."

"White doctor?" Chief Dean turned to the headman in disbelief. "What white doctor?"

"Red-beard doctor. He will come. You wait."

Mrs. Muller and Chief Dean laid the blanket over Elizabeth and looked at each other uncertainly.

Elizabeth's face had taken on a ghastly blue color. She coughed desperately. The horror-stricken girls stood by helplessly, silently grasping each other's hands for courage. Trembling, Cent moved forward and took her place with the distraught adults.

"I said," announced the headman. "He comes."

Cent looked up through her terrified tears and saw a rugged, red-bearded man running towards them with the Negrito messenger by his side.

The man knelt beside Elizabeth and motioned everyone aside. He ran his hands expertly over her body.

"Chief, I want you to pull the blanket under her as I lift her," he said. "You'll need one helper."

"Let me," cried Cent.

The doctor nodded. He ran his strong arms under the half-conscious girl, and Cent and Chief Dean pulled the blanket under her.

The doctor shook his head gravely. "Have you a pen-knife, Chief?" he asked. "It will be better than my big blade here."

"What are you planning to do?" The Chief gave a shocked look at the unknown "doctor." "I can't let you— I'm responsible for—" he cried.

"Your knife," barked the doctor. "Don't waste time. She has a broken rib and an injured lung. She can't breathe. If I puncture her pleural cavity it will release the pressure, and she'll be all right. Otherwise, she may die in ten minutes."

Chief Dean, visibly making a decision, pulled his knife from his pocket. "Send the girls to the truck, please, Mrs. Muller."

"I want to stay," said Cent clearly.

"Good," said the doctor, glancing approvingly at her. "We need you."

I mustn't faint. I mustn't faint, Cent said to herself over and over. He's going to operate on her, she thought wildly.

But the doctor grasped the knife and stood up.

"Stay with the girl," he said.

He opened the knife and walked quickly to the nearest bamboo tree. He cut a slim reed and deftly slashed it into a thin needle. Elizabeth coughed again and again as Cent stroked her hand.

"Thank God, she's not fully conscious. I'm going to plunge this needle in," he told the chief and Cent. "It will let the trapped air out and she'll be fine until we get her to the hospital. Help me hold her."

Cent gritted her teeth and prayed fervently as the doctor firmly but gently plunged his makeshift needle into Elizabeth's chest.

There was a whistle of air escaping. Almost at once Elizabeth began to breathe more normally, and her color improved.

"Now," said the doctor, "we'll carry her on the blanket and lay her on the floor of the truck. We must get her to the hospital as soon as possible."

"Could we borrow back the clothes for a mattress?" said Cent.

The headman nodded. Cent ran to the porch and grabbed up enough clothing to make a soft pad. "I'll bring them back," she said, hoping the people understood.

The two men lifted Elizabeth onto the improvised bed in the truck. Cent took her place beside Elizabeth with Mrs. Muller and the doctor. The other girls crowded silently into the truck.

"Don't worry, girls," comforted the doctor. "She's going to be all right."

The chief started the truck gently down the road. Everyone was so intent on Elizabeth that nobody saw the small dark girl who stood in the distance near the jungle opening. Nobody, that is, except the doctor, who waved to her as the truck drove out of sight.

nine

When Cent looked back on that terrible ride home she knew that she had grown up that day. Grown up in a sense that didn't involve high heels or lipstick. Grown up in a sense that dismissed the triviality of falling down in public. Grown up, grown up enough to be ashamed of her silly jealousy.

But during the ride itself Cent was conscious only of desperate prayers that Elizabeth would recover.

The doctor glanced at Cent encouragingly.

"She'll be all right," he repeated. "I'm going to leave you at the gate. You're an intelligent girl and a brave one. I'm going to tell you what to tell the doctors when you get to the hospital. Can you remember it exactly?"

"I'll remember," promised Cent, running her tongue over her dry lips.

"I'll remember too," said Mrs. Muller. "Tell us both."

"The doctor at the hospital will discover this himself but it may save him a little time. Tell him she had a tension pneumothorax."

"Tension pneumothorax," repeated Cent.

"The doctor will know what to do. She'll be up and about in a few days. You'll see."

Elizabeth opened her eyes and smiled at Cent.

Cent bit her lips. "I'm not sure I understand it, but I'll remember what you said," she promised.

They could see the gate ahead now.

"But—but why aren't you going with us to the hospital?" asked Cent.

"Please, Doctor, please don't leave us," said Mrs. Muller.

"The girl is safe now. You don't need me. I cannot go any further with you."

The doctor rose to his knees and tapped on the window, motioning the Chief to stop.

"Look here," cried Chief Dean as the doctor leaped from the truck, "you can't leave now. Who are you? You've just saved a girl's life. I can't let—"

"Don't waste time, Chief. Get the child to the hospital. It doesn't matter who I am.—Go ahead!" he shouted as

Chief Dean still didn't move. And he disappeared into the underbrush by the road.

"Call the hospital and get me an escort," Chief Dean ordered the guard when they reached the gate. "We've got an injured child. Mrs. Muller, it would be a good thing if all the girls except Cent got out here. You two can take care of Elizabeth the rest of the way now."

Later, after Elizabeth was wheeled out of surgery and put to bed, Cent sat in the waiting room with Captain and Mrs. Ellis, who had been summoned immediately.

Dr. Davis, the brisk, gray-haired surgeon, strode towards them.

"She's fine," he said, sinking down into the chair and mopping his forehead with his handkerchief. "She's remarkably fine, thanks to quick action by an expert doctor. If she had not had that effective emergency treatment we would have had a different story. Who is this doctor? I only got the barest garbled story."

"Tell Dr. Davis what you told us, Milicent."

"I don't know who he is," said Cent. "It was all so strange. He spoke with an American accent, and he was ragged and had a long red beard. I-I don't know how old he is, but he isn't really old."

"Hmmm. Did you get his name?" asked Dr. Davis.

"No, sir, he didn't tell me. Mrs. Muller and I begged him to come with us to the hospital, but he wouldn't."

"We must find him," said Mrs. Ellis. "We must find him and thank him."

"How did he happen to be there?" asked Dr. Davis.

"The Negrito headman sent for him. And he came right away. The Negritoes seemed to know him."

"I must get back to the ward," said the doctor. "But I think you will have some detective work to do to solve the mystery of the red-bearded doctor."

"Come, Milicent, I'll take you home," said Mrs. Ellis. "You've been a jolly good friend today. I know you must be beastly tired. Tomorrow we'll have to call on you to help us find this man who saved Elizabeth's life."

ten

Commander and Mrs. Hawes were waiting by the door for Cent. It was only six o'clock, a mere four hours since she had left the house with the packages of clothes for the Negritoes.

At the sight of her parents standing strong and comforting by the door Cent broke into tears, and without even saying good-by to the Ellises she ran blindly up the steps.

Mrs. Hawes put her arm around Cent. "How tired you must be. Come, dear, have a hot bath. Mrs. Muller called and told me everything, how brave you've been and all. I'll bring you your supper, some hash-brown potatoes and ginger ale, maybe?"

Cent gave her mother a squeeze and dried her eyes. She bit her lip and smiled a little at the menu. Those were her favorite foods.

"No, no thank you," she said. "I don't want anything special. And I wasn't brave."

"Do you want to tell me about it?" asked her mother.

"Not now," said Cent. "I just want to rest a while before dinner."

Mrs. Hawes chased Jemima out of the bedroom, and Cent lay across her bed alone for a few minutes.

Yesterday, thought Cent, I would have poured all this out to Mother. I would have told her how ashamed I am, and then I would have felt all right. But now, she realized with a stab of clarity, I can't. I'll have to make it right with Elizabeth all by myself.

She gave a shuddering sigh. She was tired, but her restless mind darted about, not letting her sleep. Would Elizabeth forgive her? It would serve her right if she did not.

Those words, what were those words her mother had told her look up in the dictionary? *Acrimony* and *compassion*. The dictionary was beside her bed. She pulled it over towards her.

"Acrimony," she read, "sharpness or bitterness of speech or temper, springing from a feeling of aversion or unkindness."

"Compassion," she read after flipping the pages, "pity

for suffering with a desire to help or spare."

Mrs. Hawes tapped on the door.

"Sure you don't want your supper in bed?" she asked gently.

"No, I'm coming to the table as soon as I have a bath. Mother, I know what *acrimony* and *compassion* mean now."

"Cent," said her mother, "Mrs. Muller said you seemed to feel responsible about what happened this afternoon. But you mustn't, you didn't—it's all right. Do you want to tell me about it?"

"Mrs. Muller doesn't know it all," said Cent. "It was my fault. But I'm going to make it up to Elizabeth. I'm going to find that man again, that man who saved her life. You see, he saved my life too, in a way. Suppose Elizabeth had died? I think I would have died too."

"Sure you don't want to tell me the rest?"

"I'm sure, Mother. I have to work it out myself."

Commander Hawes and Jemima were standing by the table waiting when Cent came in to dinner.

"Come on, Cent, tell us everything," cried Jemima impatiently.

"No, Jemima, Cent's tired," said Mrs. Hawes firmly.

"Oh, heck, nobody ever tells me anything," pouted Jemima.

"Tell me about the doctor, Cent," said her father. "Captain Ellis just had me on the phone. He wants your help."

"And I want to help," said Cent earnestly. "We've got to thank him somehow."

"The whole thing is unbelievable, that an unknown American doctor could be living in the jungle here. It simply makes no sense."

"But it's true, Dad. I didn't dream him up. And tomorrow I mean to find him if I can."

eleven

Cent was at the hospital long before visiting hours the next morning. She sat alone in the waiting room, not moving, not reading. She looked down at her hands in her lap. How would Elizabeth feel about her? Suppose Elizabeth refused to see her? Suppose. . . .

"Milicent?" It was Lieutenant Evans, one of the nurses.

"How is she? How is Elizabeth?" asked Cent, springing to her feet.

"She's fine," replied the nurse. "She saw you get off the bus, and she asked to see you. As a special favor to her I'm going to let you go in now before visiting hour."

"You mean she really wants to see me?" asked Cent eagerly.

"Yes," said Lieutenant Evans, leading the way down the corridor. "She even asked me not to let anyone else in until she had had a chance to see you alone. Here we are."

Lieutenant Evans ushered Cent into the small room where Elizabeth lay propped up on her high white bed.

"Here's your special visitor," said the nurse brightly. "Don't let Elizabeth talk too much." She went out, closing the door behind her.

Cent stood for a moment by the door. How frail and beautiful Elizabeth looked with her yellow hair spread out and her face white on the pillow.

"Elizabeth," Cent began, still standing by the door.

Elizabeth stretched out her hand. "Come closer, please,"

she said. "Bring the chair over here and sit near me."

Cent pulled the chair close to the bed.

"Elizabeth," she began again, biting her lip.

"Milicent, Cent," said Elizabeth, "before you say anything, I want to tell you something."

"But the nurse said you mustn't talk much," said Cent.

"It won't take me long to say it," said Elizabeth, "but I must say it. Cent, I know you think you were at fault yesterday about my fall. But you mustn't feel that way. It was my own fault."

"Your fault?" Cent broke in. "How could it be your fault when I was so mean and jealous and, and—oh, I honestly wanted to show everyone that I could swing on a vine better than you. I didn't want you to fall, not that, but I wanted to show off that I could do it better than you because you could do everything else better then I can!"

"Me do everything else better than you!" Elizabeth gave Cent an incredulous look. "Why, I can't do anything as well as you do. I've been utterly petrified of you. Everyone told me how wonderful you are and how you are such a good swimmer and make the best grades and know everything and are so popular with everybody."

"Oh, but—but—" Cent's eyes filled with tears that began to spill down her face. "That's not a bit true. And it was my fault."

"No, it wasn't. If I hadn't been such a show-off myself,

so determined to show you that I was as brave as you then I would have said no, I'm afraid to, that swings and heights frighten me most terribly. They always have."

"And I taunted you into it," Cent wept. "I did. I did."

"But don't you see, you didn't. If I had just been content to say, 'Old thing, I'm no good at this. You are, so go ahead,' then I wouldn't have caused this ghastly affair."

"I like you, Elizabeth. I want us to be friends forever. I won't ever forget this. It's going to be like a scar—like a vaccination scar. I hope I'm vaccinated against wanting always to be best."

"And me too, Cent, don't you see? Now please, please, don't cry. Let's begin now to be friends and start over again from the first day. Promise me we won't talk about it any more. We must just forget it, if we're going to be friends."

"Okay," said Cent. She pushed her hands here and there in her pockets and emptied her purse. "Have you got something I could dry my eyes on?"

"Here, take one of these tissues." Elizabeth pointed to the box beside her bed.

"Thanks," said Cent reaching for one. "I think I'll wash my face in your sink."

"Help yourself," said Elizabeth. "I want to ask you something. Couldn't you tell how panic-struck I was the day we first met there at the airstrip?"

Cent sank back in the wicker chair and stared at Elizabeth. "You're kidding," she accused.

"No, I'm not. I was utterly flummoxed. And you don't know how hard and long I practiced walking on those heels. You see, when Mummy married the Captain and we knew we would come to America to live I got dreadfully frightened that I wouldn't pass muster. I had heard American girls were so frightfully smart and advanced."

"You thought that," exclaimed Cent. "Great Scott!"

"That school I attended. Ugh, those horrid tunics we wore. Mummy finally listened to me and took me out of that hole and sent me to Paris to visit my aunt. My aunt is married to a press correspondent there, and she coached me on what her idea of a smart American would be like and supervised all my clothes."

Cent shattered into laughter. "You idiot. Did you really think all Americans were smart and chic and polished? No wonder we were all awed by you."

"I really want to have fun as you American girls do. I read about American girls every chance I had before I came. And to be truthful I didn't want to come at first. The idea of Mummy's marrying didn't strike me well to begin with."

"It must have been a sort of upheaval for you," said Cent thoughtfully.

"Some of the things I read in magazines and things about

you American girls quite terrified me," said Elizabeth.

"Such as what?" asked Cent.

"Such as going steady," confessed Elizabeth. "I thought you all would and I'd be left out."

"Nobody has ever asked me," said Cent candidly, "but I like to go to the teen dances. When you're well we can all go together. Most of the kids don't come with dates."

"Do you have dates?" asked Elizabeth.

"A boy asked me to the junior-senior prom last year," said Cent, "but he left soon after that. He was kind of funny. I didn't like him much. The ones you want to ask you, well, they ask somebody else. It always happens that way."

"Good grief, you make me feel better," sighed Elizabeth. "I was afraid I'd be a terrible wallflower with American boys and girls. Bebe and Mary don't talk about anything but boys."

"Oh, Bebe and Mary," Cent shook her head. "They're okay, but sometimes—oh, Elizabeth, I'm glad you're here. We're going to have a wonderful time. I wish you had known my friend Tammy who left not long ago."

There was a light tap on the door. It was Lieutenant Evans.

"My, everybody looks happy," she said. "But time's up now. Elizabeth needs to rest. Milicent, Captain Ellis left a call for you. He wants you to telephone him before you leave the hospital. It's important, something about the mysterious doctor."

"We didn't even get to talk about him," said Elizabeth.

"Never mind," said Cent. "I hope they've found out something about him. I'll be out first thing tomorrow with the news."

twelve

The Captain's secretary was expecting Milicent's call. "Captain Ellis wants to know if you can stop by his office this morning," she said.

"I'll come right now," said Cent. "I'm leaving the hospital."

She caught a ride with a doctor who was on his way to Base Headquarters. "The whole hospital is buzzing with the story of the mysterious doctor," he told her. "He saved the child's life, no doubt about it."

"It was funny the way he just appeared all at once. The Negritoes all seemed to know him," said Cent.

She jumped out in front of the Headquarters Building

and hurried up to the Captain's office.

"Go right in, Milicent," said the secretary. "Your father's in there with the Captain, and they're expecting you."

Cent flushed a little. It felt quite important having a special conference waiting for you.

"Ah, here she is," said her father. "Come in, Cent. We want to talk about the events of yesterday."

Mr. Gonzales, a Filipino, was there with her father and the captain.

"Hello, Mr. Gonzales," said Cent. "How are you, sir?"

"Milicent, tell Mr. Gonzales about the doctor and your experience yesterday. Perhaps he will have something to add to your story," said Captain Ellis, leaning eagerly toward Cent.

Once more Cent told the story of the strange doctor and his dramatic performance. Mr. Gonzales nodded his head as Cent unfolded the story. For many years, Cent knew, Mr. Gonzales had been the head of the Filipino employees on the Base and the trusted friend of many commanding officers. Once, Cent recalled, he came to the school and told the children Filipino folk stories.

"Do you know anything about him, Mr. Gonzales? I think he's a real hero," concluded Cent.

Mr. Gonzales gave Cent an apologetic smile. "I think I know some not very happy things about your hero, I'm afraid. If my guess is right, that is."

"What do you mean?" asked Cent in astonishment.

"Did you ever hear, Miss Milicent, about what happened here on our Naval Base during World War Two?"

"A little bit. But I never thought about it much. You see, I wasn't even born then. It must have been a long time ago."

The three men laughed.

"That's not so long ago, Milicent," said Captain Ellis. "Perhaps Mr. Gonzales had better tell you about what happened to the Americans during that time."

Mr. Gonzales closed his eyes for a moment. "It does seem a long time ago," he said. "Actually it was in 1941. The Americans had a small base here. War clouds had hung over Asia for a long time. The rise of the war party in Japan told us that sooner or later there would be trouble in our part of the world."

"Were there families here, American mothers and children, the way there are now?"

"Yes, a few. However, before the dreadful day that war really started they evacuated the families so there were only troops here that day. I can't tell you everything about the fighting as I was in the Filipino Army and stationed in the south. But this base fell to the Japanese and many brave Americans and Filipinos lost their lives in the fighting."

Cent caught her breath. How incredible to think this took place right here.

"Just before the enemy swept in most of the Americans fled to the jungle and joined the Filipino guerillas. That is, all of them fled except a few traitors who chose to stay behind here and there and collaborate with the enemy."

Mr. Gonzales cleared his throat and looked at Cent.

"It was rumored that one of these collaborators was a doctor."

"Oh, surely not—" began Cent, her heart contracting.

"Of course, there's no way yet of knowing," continued Mr. Gonzales soothingly. "It may be just a coincidence, but this is the story. Do you want to hear the rest?"

"Oh, yes," said Cent faintly. "Tell me everything."

"The day finally came when our forces, the Americans and the Filipinos, returned. The doctor was still here, so the story goes, and of course he was immediately summoned. He made no effort to clear his name. Instead he ran away."

"Ran away!" cried Cent.

"Yes, disappeared into the jungle. His name has never been cleared."

"But I don't believe for a minute it was the same man," said Cent. "Why do you think it is?"

"Because," said Mr. Gonzales, "the man who ran away had red hair."

"It must be the same man, Cent," said her father. "And we're going to send to Washington to find out his status.

We feel sure he must be listed as a traitor and a deserter."

"Where has he been all this time?" asked Cent.

"There have been stories that have drifted down to us in the barrio," said Mr. Gonzales. "Stories that the redheaded doctor was sometimes around here. I believe a halfhearted effort was made to find him. He is living here illegally, of course."

"What's his name?" asked Cent suddenly. "Do you know his name?"

"His name," said Mr. Gonzales, "if this is the man, is O'Dell. Derry O'Dell."

"Derry O'Dell," repeated Cent. "It doesn't sound like the name of a wicked man, a traitor. And I don't believe he is."

"But there is more, Miss Milicent," continued Mr. Gonzales softly. "The legends sift down our way. Sometimes I think our people are sensitive to the sound of wind. We know many things, even we people in the towns, because the jungle is so close."

Cent leaned forward. She loved the poetic way this slender, soft-voiced man spoke. "What did you hear from the jungle wind?" she asked.

"We heard that a great humanitarian was moving through the jungle. We heard that a doctor went from one remote barrio to another, giving medical treatment with homemade equipment and herb drugs to the *igorots,* our mountain people, to the Negritoes of the jungles, and to poor and ignorant Filipinos wherever he found them."

"Oh, that must be my doctor," cried Cent.

"I think so, too," said Mr. Gonzales. "He never stays anywhere very long. He goes from one place to another, never on the main roads, always through the jungle. The people back there know he is a fugitive. They'll never tell where he is. They worship him, almost. And I think, Miss Milicent, that you'll never see him again."

"No," cried Cent. "We must see him. We must thank him for what he did. He risked his safety to save Elizabeth, and now we must clear his name so he won't have to hide any more."

"But, Cent," interrupted her father, "this man is an outlaw. This is a matter for our government and no concern of yours now."

"But it is my concern," Cent insisted. "I must help him."

"Perhaps you could come with me to Jungle's Edge now, Milicent," said Captain Ellis, rising. "If your father will permit you. I want to find him as much as you do, to thank him and try to reward him for saving Elizabeth's life. We can't lose time or the rain will stop us. But remember, there is a risk here. We don't want to harm him with gratitude."

thirteen

"Could we take those clothes back to the Negritoes now, the ones we used in the truck yesterday? Chief Dean left them here in Dad's office," said Cent.

"Good idea," said Captain Ellis. "Do you think you can find the place?" he asked as they stowed the clothes in the car.

"Oh, I can find Jungle's Edge, all right, but I wonder if we can find the doctor," said Cent as they set out.

"That's the big question," said Captain Ellis. "From what Mr. Gonzales said, the doctor might have decided to move on."

"This is where we turn," said Cent after a while.

Captain Ellis eased his car along the road and came to a stop in the clearing.

They got out of the car. Cent glanced over toward the jungle where the swinging vine hung from the giant tree. The vine was idling back and forth as though someone had jumped off into the soft grass.

"There's somebody here, I'm sure of it, even if it does look deserted," she said.

With that two tiny heads appeared a few feet from them in the tall grass.

"Hello," said Cent. The children immediately disappeared. Only a bobbing head now and then and the motion of the tall grass told them that the children had run to the houses to report.

Cent and Captain Ellis walked slowly through the brown grass toward the houses. In a moment the chief appeared on his porch, and as though by signal the porches and yards of the other houses began to fill with people.

Captain Ellis strode through the grass toward the Negrito king. The sharp-eyed headman seemed to note the four gold stripes on the captain's shoulder boards and his gold-encrusted cap. This was no ordinary visitor. The headman bowed again, more deeply.

"We have come," said Captain Ellis after an exchange of greeting, "to ask you to tell us where we can find the doctor."

The Negrito stared blankly at Captain Ellis.

"Ah," he said.

The captain cleared his throat.

"My daughter, it was my daughter who was injured here yesterday. I want to thank you, and the doctor."

"Ah," repeated the headman, smiling blankly.

He is not going to tell, thought Cent suddenly. He is stalling. How can we ever find Dr. O'Dell now? From the corner of her eye Milicent saw the woman who had talked with her yesterday. Cent ran to her.

"Look," she said breathlessly, "I brought back the clothes. Show me please where the red-bearded doctor lives."

The woman looked about her, half-frightened.

"Please," begged Cent. "The Captain has come to thank him, to help him. Where is he?"

Again the woman looked about her, saying nothing.

"Is it down this path? Is that where he stays, down this path? Tell me quickly. If we don't find him today it may be too late."

"I will tell you," said the woman, haltingly. "Down that path. If you go alone I know he will not mind."

Cent turned down the narrow path. They would never hurt her, these small gentle people, and she must find the doctor no matter what the cost.

But the jungle was always fearful, and this path skirted

the edge of the immense tangle. She ran quickly. Ahead she could see that the path seemed to stop. As yet there was no house in sight.

The path did not stop. It turned abruptly toward the jungle beside a giant *dao* tree. Cent turned, and there directly before her was a high, thatched hut, half hidden in the trees.

Suddenly Cent was terribly afraid. Perhaps Captain Ellis would be angry with her for running away like this. And what would she have accomplished? Would the redheaded doctor listen to her? Would he hide? And suppose he agreed to come out of the jungle and see the Captain, how could she, one insignificant girl, clear his name?

But there was no turning back now. She bounded up the ladder to the porch.

"Hello," she called at the door.

There was a movement, a sound from the dark room.

"Doctor?" called Cent in a frightened voice.

"Yes," came a soft answer. And in the semi-dark interior Cent saw not the redheaded doctor but a fragile girl about her own age.

"What do you want with my father?" asked the girl in perfect English. "Why have you come here?"

fourteen

"I-I-," Cent, her mouth open, her face flushed, gasped.

"I know who you are," said the girl. She gave Cent a timid smile. "You're one of the American girls."

"How—how do you know?" Cent leaned against the railing of the porch and stared at the beautiful girl. She wore a faded cotton blouse and skirt and clumsy handmade leather sandals.

"I watched you. I watched all of you. You see," she said, holding out her hand, "I'm an American too."

"I don't know what to say," said Cent weakly.

"When American girls come to see you you say 'come in,

sit down.' I shall say that too. Come in, sit down."

"Thank you," said Cent. "I'd like to."

She followed the girl into the house. There were two rooms, both small. The floors were smooth, worn mahogany, and the walls were of bamboo and straw thatch. There were two chairs, both of rattan, in the outer room.

"But," said Milicent hesitantly, "I can't sit down now. I must find your father."

"Why do you want to see him?" asked the girl.

"Can't you guess?" asked Cent. "Because we want to thank him."

The girl thought a minute. "All right," she said. "I'll ask him. What is your name?"

"I'm Milicent Hawes," she said. "Tell your father I'm the redheaded girl. He'll remember."

"Oh yes," said the girl. "He told me all about you. My name is Pacita."

"Pacita," repeated Cent. "What a beautiful name. Oh," she cried suddenly, "Pacita, tell me where to find your father. I must go back quickly. Captain Ellis will be furious with me."

"Run then," said Pacita. "I will find my father and persuade him to come to you at the clearing."

Cent ran back to the clearing just as Captain Ellis began anxiously to call her name.

"Here I am," she cried, running up the path.

Captain Ellis hurried forward to meet her.

"Milicent, where have you been? Did you find the doctor? Nobody will tell me anything here."

"To his house. I've been to his house," panted Cent. "I didn't find him, but I found his daughter."

"His daughter!" exclaimed Captain Ellis.

Cent nodded. "Oh, she's beautiful. She's just about as old as Elizabeth and I are. And she has gone to find her father to ask him to come meet us here. Oh, I hope—look, look, there they come."

The red-bearded doctor and the girl stepped into the clearing. Pacita's long black hair hung about her shoulders. She pushed it back impatiently.

"Now," said Pacita, "I shall look at you together. For the first time I see two people with red hair. I have always suspected that my father was the only one in the world."

The red-bearded man let his mouth turn up in a smile.

"I told you, Pacita, that I was not the only person on earth with red hair."

"But only now do I believe you," she said. "Now I can believe anything."

Cent ran her hand through her red hair and gave a self-conscious laugh.

Captain Ellis thrust out his hand. "Dr. O'Dell? I'm Captain Ellis. You saved my daughter's life. I have come to thank you."

The ragged man stiffened at the sound of his name.

"So you know who I am," he said evenly. "So they have not forgotten down there."

"I don't know what they did or didn't forget," said Captain Ellis. "I only know that Elizabeth's mother and I will not forget that your skill saved her life. How can I thank you?"

"You have thanked me," said the doctor. "I give no bill for my services. Come, Pacita, we must go."

"But, Father," Pacita's soft face hardened. "You said, you know you said you wanted—"

"Yes, Pacita, what did he say he wanted?" cried Cent. "Tell us."

"Hush, Pacita," said her father sternly.

"No," cried Pacita, "I won't hush, because I want it too. He said last night that he wanted friends for me, American girls for friends for me since my Filipina mother is dead. He wants an American school and American shoes for me, and he wants to be an American again himself."

"Pacita!" cried out her father. "I forbid you. Stop it this instant!"

Pacita closed her mouth and dropped her head, making the dark straight hair fall over her cheek.

The two men stood silent, caught up in the drama of the moment. Cent reached out her arm and put it around Pacita's shoulder.

"I am your friend, Pacita. I am your friend, and Elizabeth will be too, won't she, Captain Ellis?" said Cent in a matter-of-fact voice.

"Of course she will," said Captain Ellis. "Doctor, may I talk with you for a moment about the matter that concerns your status and how I might be able to help you?"

The doctor turned an incredulous look on Captain Ellis. "Do you mean this? Do you know what you are saying?"

"Yes, I know what I am saying," said Captain Ellis. "But I know I must have a long talk with you, preferably with my staff lawyer in attendance."

"Captain Ellis," broke in Cent, "could Pacita come to visit us on the Base? I mean would it be all right if she came as my guest if her father will let her?"

"Oh," Pacita looked up with starry eyes, "please, Father?" Then she glanced down at her dress. "But how could I? This is the best dress I have."

"If Captain Ellis is coming back here tomorrow maybe I could come too," said Cent quickly. "Your dress is fine, but I have one that would just fit you. It's blue checked and too tight for me. I'll bring it here, and you can put it on and come home with me. Oh, we'll have a wonderful time."

Pacita looked hopefully at her father. "Oh, please, Father," she begged.

"I can't decide now, Pacita," he said. "Give me time to think. When do you want to see me again, sir? You realize you could arrest me, don't you, now that you know where I am?"

"I'm not sure I could," said Captain Ellis. "I'll have to find out what your status is, and I don't want to arrest you. I want to help you."

"I believe you," said Dr. O'Dell less coldly, "but I don't believe it will do any good. There is no one left to help me so I must help others, help them here in the jungle. I hardly know myself why I came to talk to you; except that eventually it must be settled, what I am, for my daughter's sake. The charges that may be brought against me are false. I have always been loyal to my country. I made a foolish mistake letting pride and despair turn me into a fugitive. I hope you believe me. But the jungle could swallow me again tonight," he added, his direct look locking with Captain Ellis's eyes.

"I believe your loyalty," said Captain Ellis slowly. "Don't make another foolish mistake. The jungle has served you well, but it is a prison if you can't come and go at will. I will come again tomorrow, unless the rains come today and make it impossible."

"Pacita and I go away when the rains come," said Dr. O'Dell.

"This time will you stay?" asked Captain Ellis.

"Stay and be arrested?" asked the doctor bitterly.

"Please trust me," said Captain Ellis.

The Negrito king, who was standing apart, approached them. "It will rain," he said. "It will rain soon."

The sun had gone behind a leaden bank of clouds. "Run," said Pacita, "the water will fall like a rock."

"It's true. It will, Captain," cried Cent. She gave Pacita's hand a squeeze. "The blue checked dress," she whispered. "I'll bring it to you." She hurried away to the car with Captain Ellis.

He turned the car, and they headed into the big road just as rain, blinding, lead-heavy, fierce rain began to crash from the sky.

fifteen

Cent put on her raincoat with the hood, and slipping her feet into shower shoes she stepped out into the rain. It fell hard and directly and without remission. It had rained like this for two days.

She sloshed through ankle-deep water toward the bus stop. She was on her way to visit Elizabeth. But she didn't have to wait for the bus. A car slowed down beside her. By good fortune, it was Mrs. Ellis.

"Hop in, Milicent," she invited. "Quite a rain, what? I'm on my way to the hospital now, but I came out this way to return some books to one of your neighbors."

"I'm going to the hospital too," said Cent. "I'm sorry to get the car so wet."

"No bother," said Mrs. Ellis. "I believe everything here will be sopping before long, no matter how hard we try otherwise."

"Is Captain Ellis going out to see Dr. O'Dell today?" asked Cent. "My father said I couldn't go out there again, not in all this rain. But he said he would get the dress out to Pacita as soon as they could get through. They couldn't make it yesterday."

"So I heard," said Mrs. Ellis. "Yes, I think my husband is going to try again today. He and the staff lawyer plan to attempt the trip. The roads must be almost completely under water."

"Yesterday I went to visit Elizabeth and told her everything about my trip to Jungle's Edge. We both want Pacita to visit us. Don't you, Mrs. Ellis?" asked Cent.

"It is something to consider," said Mrs. Ellis noncommitally. That's just the way my mother sounded, thought Cent.

At the hospital Cent offered to wait in the waiting room while Mrs. Ellis visited Elizabeth.

"Oh no, come on with me. We'll trudge in together. She'll be dying to see you."

Elizabeth was sitting up on the side of her bed in a red Chinese silk robe.

"Oh, how gorgeous," exclaimed Cent.

"My step—I mean, my father brought it to me. It's

pretty, isn't it? Did you select it, Mummy?" asked Elizabeth, glancing guardedly at her mother.

"Indeed not," said Mrs. Ellis. "I never saw it before. It is lovely on you. How are you feeling, dear?"

"Wonderful," said Elizabeth. "The doctor says I may come home. He wants to talk to you about it."

"Home? Already?" exclaimed Mrs. Ellis in such a shocked voice that Elizabeth and Cent looked at each other and laughed aloud.

"Honestly, Mummy, you sound as if you didn't want me to come home."

"No, no," said Mrs. Ellis, laughing at herself, "I'm just surprised, that's all."

"Oh, that would be divine," said Cent. "Now if Pacita comes we can all see each other as much as we like."

"I thought of that too, and I was almost hoping she couldn't come until I'm well. Oh, Mummy, I have a really wizard idea. Supersonic wizard," she cried, jumping off the side of the bed and standing before her mother.

"Elizabeth, Elizabeth," cautioned her mother. "Are you supposed to be out of bed?"

"Certainly, Mummy. I walked all around the hospital this morning. I even saw the new babies through the glass windows. Anyhow, this supersonic wizard idea. You know how much space we have in our house?"

"Yes?" said Mrs. Ellis, looking up at Elizabeth.

"Well then, when I come home from the hospital why can't Milicent and Pacita come and stay with me at our quarters, like a house party?"

"I don't think it sounds feasible at this point," said Mrs. Ellis pausing a moment. "The Captain said that the possibility of a visit from the girl was mentioned, but he felt it was unwise."

"Why?" cried Elizabeth, her face coloring. "Why did he say *that?*"

There was a tap on the door. "Hi, Queen Bess." It was Bebe and Mary, each carrying an enormous bunch of gardenias.

"Only two visitors at a time," reminded one of the nurses' aides who was pushing a cart of books down the corridor.

"Right you are," said Mrs. Ellis, rising.

"Oh, don't go, Mrs. Ellis. We don't want to run you off. Only Cent. She's monopolizing Elizabeth," said Bebe giving Cent an affectionate grimace.

"I guess we know when we're not wanted, don't we, Mrs. Ellis?" said Cent, poking her chin out at Mary and Bebe.

"Good riddance," said Mary in a loud whisper.

"I must go and speak to the doctor now in any case," said Mrs. Ellis smiling.

"So long, party-crashers," said Cent.

"I don't think I shall ever get accustomed to American girls," said Mrs. Ellis shaking her head and laughing. "You quite terrify me."

"Oh, we only talk that way when we really like each other," said Cent. "When your friends are too polite, then you have something to worry about."

sixteen

Cent waited impatiently for her father to come in from work that afternoon. He promised to tell her any news that the Captain might bring back from Jungle's Edge.

The rain had continued to pour unceasingly. Cent cleaned up her room and dug through her closet looking for clothes that might fit Pacita.

At five o'clock Commander Hawes ran in from the carport, dripping water from cap-cover to overshoes. The porch was awash with wet raincoats and dripping umbrellas.

Cent was standing eagerly by the door.

"What happened at Jungle's Edge? How is Pacita? Is she going to come visit here?" Cent shot the questions at her father.

"Hold on, hold on," begged her father, stripping off his wet wraps. "I'll tell you in a moment."

Cent waited impatiently until her father settled down in an easy chair.

"I went to Jungle's Edge myself," he said.

"You did," said Cent in surprise. "Why didn't you let me go too?"

"Too much rain, too much serious business, and because your mother said no."

"What about Pacita?" asked Cent. "What did her father decide?"

"Frankly, her father is against it now. And so am I. It would be very hard to get her here. Captain Ellis and Lieutenant Jenkins, the new lawyer, and I had a terrible time getting out there today."

Cent's face clouded. "I don't see why it would be so hard to get her here. You got back yourself. Did you see Pacita? Did you give her the dress?"

"Yes, I saw her, and I gave her the dress. She was delighted with it. We went to their house. Funny thing, you'd think it would leak, but it didn't. It was very cosy."

"I still don't see why you didn't bring Pacita back with you," persisted Cent. "You're hedging, Dad."

"Cent, don't push me too hard. Don't force this thing. It may take a week or more to get an answer to the dispatch we sent to Washington in her father's behalf."

"Oh, you mean you've already started things going to clear his name?" asked Cent excitedly.

"Look here, Cent," said her father wrinkling his forehead. "Don't get the wrong impression about this. There is no foregone conclusion that we can clear his name. This man is probably on record as being a deserter and a collaborator. He is in serious trouble as far as the government is concerned."

Cent looked past her father at the open window. The rain, pencil-straight, bullet hard, was still falling heavily. How would it be, she thought, to live in a straw hut at the edge of the jungle with a hunted father?

"We've got to clear him, Dad. We owe it to him. At least I owe it to him. What if Elizabeth had died? Would I have wanted to live feeling responsible for it? Don't you see?"

"Don't get overdramatic about this, Milicent," said her father irritably. "I want to help them too. But remember, my first duty is to the Navy, and so is Captain Ellis's. For this reason you girls must not get involved with Pacita. Keep the personal element out of it."

"But Dad, that's not right! I can't help being involved with Pacita. I'm already involved." Cent faced her father stormily.

"I don't want to discuss it any more," said Commander Hawes with exasperation. "I've told you I'll do what I can, but I am making no promises."

seventeen

The next day Elizabeth came home from the hospital, but the doctor ordered that there must be no visitors on homecoming day.

The following afternoon Cent stopped by the Navy Exchange and bought a small box of candy for Elizabeth and padded down to deliver it.

Elizabeth met her at the door in a pair of shorts and a loud shirt. "I've gone American," she said.

"You look fine," said Cent, stripping off her raincoat. "I've brought you a present."

"Wizard, let's eat it," said Elizabeth leading the way to her big high-ceilinged bedroom. "I'll play you the record

Bebe and Mary sent me."

"I've missed you," said Cent settling down on the bed.

"Have some candy," said Elizabeth.

"I mustn't. Let's see if I can bear to watch you eat it. Did you ask your parents about Pacita?"

"My stepfather doesn't want her to come, I have concluded," said Elizabeth with annoyance. "I don't understand."

"My father's the same way," said Cent. "We had a sort of fight about it. He doesn't think we ought to get emotionally involved or some such thing. Why don't you beg your stepfather to let her come?"

"I don't think I could ever beg my stepfather for anything," said Elizabeth. "Do you think I'm frightfully odd to feel this way?" She turned a troubled face to Cent.

"Why do you feel that way?" asked Cent. "Don't you like him? He seems pretty nice to me."

"I don't know why," admitted Elizabeth. "He is nice. Too nice sometimes. I always think he felt I was—well a sort of fly in the ointment when he married Mummy."

"I don't see why you feel that way," said Cent. "Maybe you just think about it too much. Maybe you're sensitive. I loved that red robe he brought you."

"Me too," admitted Elizabeth. "But I felt that he thought he ought to. And Mummy is so anxious for us to get on, you see, that I can't quite. I can't even call him Dad. It sticks in my throat."

"What you need is to have a good fight with him," said Cent. "Oh, I get so mad with my father sometimes. He's just being so—so *arbitrary* about this thing. Elizabeth, suppose they find that Dr. O'Dell is a deserter and they put him in jail? Then what will become of Pacita?"

"I don't know," said Elizabeth sadly.

Cent stared at her feet, propped on the bedpost. "Maybe we'll know something tomorrow," she said.

The dispatch arrived from Washington the next day, and that afternoon Cent learned the probable fate of Dr. O'Dell.

She was in her room talking to Molly, who was leaving the next day for a trip to Hong Kong. They were putting coral polish on their toenails and talking about the trip. Cent listened restlessly for her father, who was due home from the office any minute.

She heard his car drive in.

"Where's Cent?" she heard him ask.

"In her room. She's got company," said Jemima. "Want me to go get her? They won't let me in."

"Don't bother her," Cent heard her father say.

Molly was only halfway through her toes.

"Here," said Cent briskly, "let me help you." She knew her father must have news about Dr. O'Dell. Molly blew her toes dry and stood up.

"I guess I'd better be going," she said. "Mother gets nervous about the packing."

"Have a good trip," said Cent walking with her to the door a little too quickly.

Her guest gone, she raced expectantly to her father's room and tapped on the door.

"Did you want me? Is it good news?" asked Cent hopefully.

"I'm sorry to have to tell you this, Cent. It is what I feared all along. Dr. O'Dell is listed as a deserter and a probable enemy collaborator. Captain Ellis is ordered to ensure the man's presence in the area until further instructions."

"What does that mean? Not—" Cent broke off in despair.

"I'm afraid," said Commander Hawes, "that it means that Dr. O'Dell is subject to arrest, and could even be held in the brig if necessary. I know how badly you feel about this, Cent, but there is nothing I can do about it."

eighteen

Cent walked back to her own room and sat dejectedly on the side of the bed. Her mother was at a tea party. She wished she could see Elizabeth. Dully she went over in her mind what Dad had told her. She heard the doorbell ring. Let somebody else answer it, she thought.

The rain had stopped, but there was no sun. A penetrating dampness made her shiver. Celie tapped on her door.

"Cent, Elizabeth is here."

Elizabeth! Cent jumped from her bed.

"Here I am," called Elizabeth from the living room.

"How marvelous!" cried Cent. "Come on back to my room."

"I've just come from the clinic," said Elizabeth, settling down. "I'm all well now. Mummy dropped me off here while she goes to some tea nearby. Did the dispatch come?"

"Oh, it's terrible, Elizabeth. They've got to arrest Dr. O'Dell."

"No, no! Are you sure?"

Cent nodded. "Dad said they were ordered to keep Dr. O'Dell around until they decided what to do next. That could mean hold him in jail if necessary."

Elizabeth and Cent lay propped on the two beds staring glumly at the dripping windows.

"It's dreadful the way things happen," said Elizabeth miserably. "To think he might be put in jail just because he saved my life."

"Dad didn't say they had to put him in jail," said Cent. "He just said they had to be sure he didn't run away. Dad feels terrible about it, I know. But it still makes me mad. All those horrible rules."

"Maybe we could get through to Dr. O'Dell and warn him somehow," said Elizabeth thoughtfully.

"But how?" said Cent.

"Cent, come down here a moment," called her father from the foot of the stairs.

"Maybe he's thought of something," cried Cent, jumping up. The girls raced together down the stairs.

"I've just telephoned your father, Elizabeth. I think we

have a plan that might work. On thinking it over further we believe it might be a good idea to have Pacita come visit here."

"Oh, Dad," cried Cent. "I knew you'd see it our way. You do understand how much we want to see her!"

"Wait a minute. I think I ought to explain that this is not entirely for your sakes, girls. You see, if Pacita is here with us, her father is not likely to abandon her. And we don't want to arrest him formally. It would make all kinds of trouble and publicity, something we would like to spare him. And we're instructed to 'ensure his presence.' I believe the man is innocent, and there must be some way to clear his name; but to do that we *must* persuade him to stay here. What better way could we do it?"

"Dad, you are a genius!" cried Cent, throwing her arms around his neck.

"Oh, I say, this is splendid," exclaimed Elizabeth. "When will she come?"

"Tomorrow, I hope. Of course it depends on her father, but I hardly think he will refuse; especially since you girls want her so much. That still worries me a little, incidentally." He rubbed his forehead and looked at the girls. "There could be an adverse ruling. It would be harder for you if Pacita were here."

Cent stood in front of her father. "I think you don't

know I'm not a little child any more, Dad," she said evenly. "You have to risk something for friendship."

Commander Hawes looked at his daughter and smiled. "Good girl, Cent."

"Oh, here's Mummy," said Elizabeth. "I'll have to alert her about the house party."

Early in the afternoon Cent's mother drove her to the Ellises' quarters. At the door, Cent sat for a moment without moving.

"Mother," she said, picking her words with care, "will you be hurt if I don't get in touch with you all the time? I want to feel that I really am away on a house party. I want to help Pacita, and I want to sort of live here for a few days. Don't let Jemima call me up, will you?"

"All right, dear, I understand. I won't be hurt."

"Thanks, Mother," said Cent giving her mother a good-by kiss.

Elizabeth was waiting for her. "Come and see," she invited. "Everything is ready. I've got an extra bed in my room. Do you think she'll come?"

"Oh, she'll come," said Cent. "This is the biggest bedroom I ever saw. It's four times as big as the cubby hole Jemima and I share."

"Don't forget this used to be a hospital," said Elizabeth. "This room must have been a ward."

"You know something, Elizabeth? This must have been the hospital where Pacita's father was stationed," said Cent. She glanced at the window. "Look, here they come. See, they're just turning the corner."

"Come on," said Elizabeth, "let's run to meet her."

nineteen

The rugged little truck drew into the driveway of the Ellises' quarters. Pacita was in the back seat beside Commander Hawes. Captain Ellis gave her his hand, and Pacita, feather light, stepped gracefully to the ground.

Elizabeth and Cent, now that she was here, were suddenly tongue tied.

"*Mabuhuy,*" said Pacita, smiling.

"*Mabuhuy,*" replied Cent. "That means 'hello' here in the Philippines, Elizabeth. Hi, Dad."

"Everybody happy now?" asked Commander Hawes.

"Yes, yes," said Cent and Elizabeth together.

"Oh, very happy," said Pacita, gazing at the big house before her.

"Come on," said Elizabeth. "We'll take your baggage."

Pacita opened her hands in an empty gesture. "I have nothing but myself," she said, glancing down at the blue checked dress.

"So much the better," said Cent heartily. "Then there's nothing to carry."

Pacita, Elizabeth, and Cent sat down in the living room and sipped a coke. Now that they were all together, now that each had overcome her father's resistance, there seemed little to say.

"How pretty it is here," said Pacita, looking about at the elegantly furnished tropical room. Into Cent's mind there flashed a memory of the crude little jungle house.

"Let's take advantage of this slack," said Cent. "Let's go for a walk and show Pacita around the Base. Are you well enough now, Elizabeth?"

"I'll telephone Mummy and ask. She's at the Red Cross office today. I'm sure it will be fine if we don't go too far."

"Maybe we'll run into some of our friends," said Cent. "Won't they be surprised to see Pacita! Nobody knew you were coming, Pacita, except Elizabeth and me. And we certainly had our fingers crossed that your father would say yes."

"Not even I knew it," said Pacita, "until the last minute. There was a long talking between the men before he agreed. And I found it hard to understand since he has many times lately said he wished I had some American girl friends."

"Oh, fathers are hard to understand," said Cent.

She glanced down at her white bermudas and then at Pacita's dress. "I brought along some things I've outgrown. Would you like to try a pair of shorts?"

Pacita smiled. "I like my new dress. I am not accustomed to wearing shorts. But my shoes—" she looked ruefully at her rough sandles.

"That's no problem," said Cent. "We all wear shower shoes in the rainy season."

"And I have an extra pair," said Elizabeth. "I'll get them for you. Mummy said I could go walking, but not very far."

Down the shady old street the girls strolled, arm in arm. Pacita glanced proudly at her new shoes and looked from side to side. The Captain's quarters were near the center of the Base, not on the hill with the other quarters.

"Look who's coming," said Cent. "Isn't that Bebe and Mary? Hi!"

"Hi, yourselves," Bebe called. "How's the invalid?"

"I'm not an invalid any more," answered Elizabeth, "but I suppose I shouldn't go any further. I want you to meet Pacita, Pacita O'Dell."

"Pacita O'Dell," exclaimed Bebe. "Then it's your father who—oh, how wonderful you could come. Have you come to visit Cent?"

"She's visiting me," said Elizabeth. "So is Cent. They're both staying at my house."

Bebe and Mary exchanged an embarrassed glance. They, as well as everyone else on the Base, had now heard about the renegade doctor and his beautiful daughter. But visiting Elizabeth? This was a surprise. What did you say to a girl whose father was involved in such a messy affair?

"I think it's going to rain again," said Bebe awkwardly.

"Yes, and I've lost my umbrella, and Mother says that if I lose another one I'm going to have to stay home until the rainy season is over," said Mary a trifle too loudly.

"In the jungle," said Pacita, "we make umbrellas with palm fronds."

"How clever," said Elizabeth.

"Oh, yes, I've seen them in the market," said Mary.

"Come to my house and visit us, won't you?" asked Elizabeth as they reached her corner.

"I can't," said Mary. "I'm on my way to my music lesson, and Bebe's mother is going to pick us up there. We'll come another time, won't we, Bebe?"

Mrs. Ellis had returned when the girls reached the house. Elizabeth introduced Pacita to her mother.

"I think everyone should take a rest," said Mrs. Ellis. "The doctor said Elizabeth must not overtax herself, and I'm sure Pacita is tired. Elizabeth, you lie down on my bed, and Pacita can go to Elizabeth's room, and you, Cent—"

Mrs. Ellis glanced around.

"Let me curl up here on the porch if that's all right with you, Mrs. Ellis. I'm not a bit tired. I want to look at the British magazines over there on the table."

"Right you are," said Mrs. Ellis. "Not a peep now until dinner time."

"Milicent," Mrs. Ellis whispered, slipping out onto the porch where Cent lay reading after the house was quiet. "How are things going with Pacita? Do you think she will be overwhelmed with our more civilized ways?"

"Everything's fine, Mrs. Ellis. I thought about that too. But she seems so at home. So far she fits right in, making everyone else at ease."

"I hope the food won't be too jolly strange for her at dinner. After all, living the way she has she probably hasn't had much chance to learn about table manners. I warned Elizabeth that we must make her feel at ease."

The warning was not necessary. At dinner Pacita handled her knife and fork with assurance. After dinner the girls turned down Captain Ellis's invitation to go to a movie. It was raining again, and both Elizabeth and Cent were eager to slip into pajamas and persuade Pacita to tell them about her exotic life. And somehow they had to try to think of some way to help Dr. O'Dell. The best way to begin was by finding out more about him.

Mrs. Ellis had laid a pair of Elizabeth's pajamas on the foot of Pacita's bed.

"I never wore pajamas before," said Pacita. "At the mission school I wore a long white nightgown."

"At the mission school? I didn't know you went to school, Pacita," said Cent in surprise.

"After my mother died when I was very small the mission school in the north kept me for several years. Later when I was bigger I only stayed there part of the year, while my father went deep into the jungle to heal the sick. If I had not been to school I would not know how to read and write, and speak Spanish," said Pacita.

"You speak Spanish?" asked Elizabeth.

"*Sí, señorita,*" laughed Pacita. "Are you surprised? The teachers at the mission, they are such good women. They taught me table manners and how to make people at ease with little sayings about the weather and pretty flowers."

"Pacita, you are amazing," said Cent shaking her head.

"They did this because they are good and because my father has done much for them. They did not ask too closely why he lived a roaming, fugitive life."

Pacita looked around. "I myself did not know why we were always the roving ones, the different ones, until Father explained it to me a few years ago. And to think it all began right here in this very house."

"Then you knew this was the old hospital," said Elizabeth in surprise.

"Yes, Father told me. Every year we come and stay for

a while at our little house at Jungle's Edge, and Father helps the Negritoes. News comes to them about things that happen here on the Base, and they tell my father."

"We want to help you, Pacita," said Cent. "Goodness, listen to that rain!"

"Ooops, the lights are flickering," said Elizabeth. "How can we help you, Pacita?"

"I don't know," said Pacita somberly.

"I wish you would tell us—well, everything about your father. Maybe if all of us worked very hard on thinking about it we could think of something to help," said Cent.

"I don't mean to sound silly," said Elizabeth, half serious, "but if we concentrate very hard right here on the spot maybe the spirits or poltergiests or whatever will come to our aid. But—"

There was a gust of wind. The lights flickered, blinked, flared up, then total darkness.

"Ghosts!" squealed Cent.

"Poltergeists," cried Elizabeth.

"Ohhhhhh," Pacita drew in her breath.

"Everything all right, girls?" came the reassuring voice of Captain Ellis. "Here's a candle."

Elizabeth fumbled her way to the door. "Oh, thank you, sir," she said.

"You girls look scared to death," said Captain Ellis, surveying the three faces in the candlelight. "It's just a power failure. It happens often in the heavy rains."

The wind blustered around the house while the girls settled uneasily back on their beds in the candlelight.

Cent wrapped her bedspread around herself. "I'm almost chilly," she shuddered. "All this talk about poltergeists."

"Come over to my bed. We can't hear each other talk over the noise of the rain," said Elizabeth.

"Let's push two beds together and all get close to each other," said Cent.

Pacita and Cent pushed the two nearest beds together, and the three girls curled up while the lone candle sputtered on the bedside table.

twenty

"I will tell you about my father now," said Pacita. "I am more used to the light of a single candle than I am to the bright lights of your house."

Her black hair hung down her back, brushed away from her delicate face. She looked fragile and unreal, bundled in the big white bedspread.

"Where shall I begin?" she said, frowning a little. "I will begin by telling you my father is innocent of the charges. He was not a collaborator and a deserter, no matter what they say."

"I knew it," said Cent. "I knew he was innocent."

"Now all we have to do is prove it," said Elizabeth.

"Tell us everything, Pacita. What really happened. Cent and I are utterly green about this."

"Then I will tell you the story exactly as my father told it to me. He was an American Navy doctor, sent here for duty in 1940. He described to me how it was here. The Base, before it was bombed, was very different from the way it is now."

"It's hard to believe this place was bombed," said Elizabeth.

"Oh yes, the Japanese bombed it when they bombed Pearl Harbor, then and many times again," said Pacita.

"Dad told me about it," said Cent. "He said this house and the old Spanish fort are all that is left of the old Base."

"My father said the same," continued Pacita. "In those days my father was a young doctor, a bachelor. He liked the gay life here very much. There was a little officers' club he told me about, and the ships from the United States fleet came in and out. There was much pleasure in the life. But soon they feared the Japanese were planning war, and luckily they sent home the women and children before the terrible war began. So on the December day when the Japanese came flying in, bombing the Americans, my father, one of the few doctors, was a most essential man."

"Of course he was," agreed Elizabeth.

"There were not many Americans left on the Base, and

the attempts to defend it ended as soon as the Japanese landed tanks. The commanding officer and many others had been killed in the bombing. The hospital, this very building we are in, was running over with wounded men. My father had a big red cross put on top of the roof in hopes the bombers would spare it."

"It must have worked," said Cent. "It's still standing."

"When it was certain the Japanese were going to land and nothing could stop them, the few men remaining decided to retreat and join our troops to the south."

"Your father, what did your father do?" cried Cent, leaning forward on her elbows, hypnotized by the grim story told in the eerie candlelight.

"He did not retreat. How could he? He said he would stay with our wounded and take his chances on capture."

"But the other doctors? What did they do?" asked Elizabeth, clasping her hands.

"There was only one other doctor left. He begged my father to come with him to the jungle, but my father refused. That doctor was killed in guerilla fighting later."

"Why didn't the men who escaped take the wounded men from the hospital with them?" asked Cent.

"There was no place to take them, and besides they were so seriously wounded that it would have been certain death. So my father stayed behind with the hospital and one Filipino pharmacist, Leon, to assist him. Then the Japanese surged in, taking over our Base." Pacita paused.

"What happened then? What did they do to your father?" asked Elizabeth, clasping and unclasping her hands.

"At first they came to the hospital and spoke roughly to him and threatened him, but they realized it would be valuable to have a doctor there for their wounded as their own doctor was killed. So they put a guard around the hospital and let my father continue as a doctor."

"What finally happened to the wounded men?" asked Cent.

"Some of them died, and some got better and escaped. At last my father felt free to attempt his escape with the last patients. It was now that the message came to him through Leon."

"What message?" asked Cent.

"It was a message from an underground agent. He wanted Father to stay there, to steal drugs and collect information for the guerilla fighters. An underground movement had sprung up through the island, and the leader wanted Father to stay where he was as he could serve better that way."

"But this put your father in great danger, didn't it?" asked Elizabeth.

"Of course," said Pacita. "He had to make it appear that he was friendly to the Japanese. This way he could get information. Also, they supplied him with medicines for the sick Japanese. Medicine was impossible to get in those terrible days for our jungle fighters. Father was able to steal drugs from the Japanese and get them to our fighters through Leon, who got them to another agent."

"Oh, Pacita! Don't other people know this, know the good your father did?" asked Cent.

"They are dead, scattered, and unknown. And of course, the agents didn't use their own names. These were underground fighters he dealt with, and he never saw them himself. Later, Father tried to find out if there was anyone who could vouch for him, but the effort failed. He took only one safeguard for his future, and in the end it failed."

"What was it? What did he do?" asked Cent excitedly.

"There was a record. Leon kept it like a pharmacist's logbook. It had the code names of agents, and the amounts of drugs Father was able to steal for the guerillas. You know when doctors write out prescriptions they use a kind of code for pharmacists. That's the way Leon kept his record, using that code. The Japanese would think it was a medical log in case they ever found it. But the book had in it enough record to clear them in the end."

"What happened to it?" cried both girls at once.

"It was destroyed."

"Oh, no!"

"Yes, they kept it locked in the safe. You see, Father

was allowed to keep things like narcotics locked up, away from the patients. Father continued to supply information and drugs to our jungle forces through Leon and his Filipino agents. When the Japanese were about to lose the war they became very vigilant with Father. Leon had the book."

"But these people, these jungle fighters, didn't they know about your father?" persisted Cent.

"It was all so secret. You can see the danger of having anyone know. But the book had names and dates which could be verified. Father was kept under close guard by the Japanese while ministering to the wounded as the American bombers zoomed overhead that day. He says the Japanese would have shot him except that he was the only doctor.

" 'I have put the book in the safe place,' Leon managed to whisper to Father. Then Leon was called away into another wing, just before the bomb hit."

"Hit the hospital?" cried out Elizabeth.

"Yes, one wing was destroyed. Father realized that this moment of confusion was his chance to get Leon and escape to a hiding place until the Americans landed. He ran to the damaged wing to find Leon, but Leon was dead. And the blazing rubble from the bomb damage cut off the entrance to the secret tunnel where he meant to hide."

"The secret tunnel!" exclaimed Cent. "What secret tunnel?"

"Oh, don't you know of the tunnel?" asked Pacita in surprise.

"We never heard of it," cried Elizabeth. "Tell us, oh tell us! You mean a secret tunnel in this house?"

twenty-one

"Yes, the old Spanish tunnel," said Pacita, looking from one to the other. "I thought of course you would know of it. Father said this building was built on the foundation of an old Spanish fort, and that Leon showed him the tunnel entrance. The Japanese never knew of it."

"I never heard of such a thing," said Cent, running both her hands through her hair in her excitement.

"They got the drugs out through the tunnel, and the messages to the guerillas. They would put the things there for the agents to pick up. The entrance was under a stone in the floor. It's a long tunnel with an exit out in the jungle somewhere."

"Where could it be? How could one get into it?" asked Elizabeth, looking around as if to find it in her bedroom.

Pacita thought a minute. "The entrance was under the part of the building that was bombed."

"That would be on the east side," said Cent. "Dad told me the east half of the old building was destroyed."

"That must be where our terrace is now," said Elizabeth. "And it's all covered in cement now."

"Then the entrance to the old tunnel could be down below the terrace," said Pacita.

"Maybe not," cried Cent rising to her knees and letting the bedcover fall off her shoulder in her excitement. "There might be a blocked-up entrance to the tunnel out there in your garden, Elizabeth. Tomorrow morning we can go out there and dig around and maybe find it. Oh, I wish we could go right now!"

"Think of it," exclaimed Elizabeth, "finding an ancient tunnel in my garden! But what we're trying to do is help Dr. O'Dell," she added. "I suppose finding old tunnels wouldn't solve anything for him."

"Anyhow, when morning comes I intend to have a look, rain or no rain," declared Cent. "But keep on with the story, Pacita."

"Father was badly burned trying to rescue Leon," she said slowly.

"But what about the book? Didn't he try to find the book?" asked Elizabeth.

"There was no use. The safe was blown to bits. You see, the safe was right by the tunnel entrance, and that was near where the bomb hit. All was fire and smoke, but Father knew the Americans would soon land and he would be reunited with his own people. He says now that everything would have been all right even without the book if he hadn't been so ill."

"Poor man," murmured Cent.

"If you knew my father you would know what a fearless man he is, really careless of his life. He's not the kind of man to worry about his own safety. If he had been he would not have come out of the jungle that day when Elizabeth fell. If he had been the careful sort he would not have played the dangerous game of spying for the guerillas without any more safeguard than a little book. I don't think it had ever occurred to him that he would be doubted any more than it occurs to him to be afraid of the weather or the jungle people."

"But didn't he tell the authorities, about his real role, that he wasn't a collaborator?" asked Elizabeth.

"He tried to. He never got a chance to see the commanding officer. Actually, he was so sick with the burn and so grieved over the death of Leon that when his own people doubted him, it was too much. He had lived all those years in the constant peril of being detected by the Japanese, and this was his reward."

"What did he do?" asked Cent breathlessly.

"He says his mind is not clear on what exactly he did do. I suppose you could say he 'blacked out.' Anyhow, he walked off into the jungle, turning his back on civilization."

"It's too bad he did that, but I understand the way he felt," said Cent.

"I can too. When you are sick things look different," said Elizabeth.

"What did your father do at first in the jungle?" asked Cent.

"Father became delirious and wandered in the jungle until he was found by some kind Filipinos who nursed him back to health. It was there he met my mother."

"Please tell us about your mother," begged Elizabeth.

"My mother had a sad story," said Pacita. "Father says I look like her, but I do not remember her. Her barrio, her village, had been burned early in the war when she was only a young girl. She was orphaned. The kind people, they are now dead, who took my father in had given her a home. When father got well they were married. They lived in a remote barrio.

"Gradually, Father began to minister to the local people, the Negritoes and the other Filipinos who lived back in the mountains. After I was born my mother lived for only two years. When she died my father took me to the mission.

For many years the teachers at the mission helped me. In the good weather I have gone with my father. He loves the people and has many friends in the jungle, and so have I."

"Do you love the jungle, Pacita?" asked Cent.

"Yes, but my dream is to go to America and learn to be a nurse. Then I want to come back here and serve my people here. For I am Filipina too, and I could bring good things from one people to another," said Pacita simply.

"Oh, Pacita," cried Elizabeth, tears in the corners of her eyes. "I want you to do it too."

Cent reached over and grasped Pacita's hand. "There will be a way. There must be a way to clear your father and make your dream come true."

twenty-two

It was hard to sleep with the exciting thoughts running through her mind. Cent tossed and crumpled the covers as she tried to put the events of the jumbled story into order in her mind.

Finally she heard the deep regular breathing of Pacita and Elizabeth in their beds. They were asleep. She turned over again, giving her pillow a thump. The house was deeply silent, deathly dark. The rain was hitting the roof fitfully, accenting the silence.

She drowsed, almost asleep, dreamily groping through rubble searching for a black book. She was startled awake by a roar. No, it was a hum. There was light. She sat up, half awake. The electric power was on again. Elizabeth had turned off the bedroom switch, but the hall light, the bathroom light, and the refrigerator all began to live again.

She straightened her covers and lay down again.

I have put the book in the safe place. I have put the book in the safe place. Did that have to mean the safe? Did Leon really say "safe place"? Or was that just Pacita's way of saying it?

But suppose he did say "the safe place"? Suppose that didn't mean the safe? Suppose it simply meant a place where the book would be safe? Why wouldn't *the* safe place mean *a* safe place, and why wouldn't a safe place be the tunnel where they hid the drugs? *Why wouldn't it?*

Cent sat up in bed and peered through the darkness at Pacita's bed. In her half-awake state the idea seemed sizzling hot. She wanted to share it. But Pacita was asleep, the white cover rising rhythmically with her deep breathing.

It was almost morning when Cent finally fell into a restless sleep, a sleep invaded by dreams of struggling down long Arabian Nights' tunnels where dogs with eyes as big as saucers guarded jewel-encrusted books.

It was almost ten o'clock when Cent opened her eyes again. Pacita and Elizabeth were sitting up in bed whispering. The rain had slowed down to a gentle misting, but it was a clammy gray day, a day for whispering.

"Hi," whispered Cent. "Why are we all so quiet?"

"For your sake, dear," said Elizabeth. "We didn't want to awaken you."

Cent sat up and yawned defiantly. "I'm hungry," she announced.

There was a tap on the door.

"Elizabeth." It was Mrs. Ellis. "Breakfast is ready. I'm going shopping this morning, so I won't be here."

The girls dressed quickly and splashed water on their faces, ran combs through their hair, and followed Elizabeth to the dining room. The long table was set with three places at one end, and the little serving maid was standing by to bring their meal.

"How did you two sleep?" asked Elizabeth.

"Wonderfully," said Pacita. "What a soft bed."

"I didn't get to sleep for ever so long," said Cent, cutting into her pineapple. "I kept thinking and thinking about something." She put down her fork. "Now I can't remember what I was thinking, but there was an idea I had sort of in my sleep."

Cent put her finger tips on her forehead.

"Now I remember," she cried. "Pacita, what *exactly* did Leon say to your father when he told him he had put the book away? Did he say 'I have put it in the safe,' or did he say 'I have put it in the safe place'?"

Pacita laid down her fork and thought a minute. "When Father told me the story I think he said that Leon said 'I have put the book in the safe place.' "

"But," Cent leaned forward, her elbows on the table, "couldn't he have meant *a* safe place? A place that's safe, not *the* safe!"

"Rather!" cried Elizabeth. "Maybe he never meant to put it in the safe at all! Perhaps he didn't put it in the safe but somewhere else—"

"The tunnel!" burst out Pacita and Cent in one breath.

"Of course, it might have been put in the tunnel," cried Elizabeth, her face rosy with excitement.

"And if Leon *did* put it in the tunnel, it's probably still there!" shouted Cent, jumping up from the table.

"Come on," cried Elizabeth, throwing down her napkin. "Let's go out to the garden. Maybe there's a rocked-over entrance out there under the shrubbery."

twenty-three

The ground was soupy wet.

"At least it isn't pouring," said Elizabeth thankfully, looking up at the dreary sky which drooped over them.

The rain had made the shrubs in the garden grow. Long shoots stuck out from the hibiscus bushes, and the usually trim gardenia bushes were ragged and unkempt with overgrown branches.

The girls padded out into the center of the yard and looked back at the house, trying to visualize it in flames and destruction. All they could see was a weathered stucco house of odd proportions with a large cement terrace, partially surrounded by trellises of purple bougainvillea and sampaguita. The ground around the terrace was open, flat, ragged lawn.

Silently and slowly the girls walked around the garden studying the ground, examining over and over the dark areas below the low shrubs. There was nothing to indicate a covered-over tunnel entrance.

"The entrance must be right under the cement of this terrace," said Pacita hopelessly.

They turned back to the terrace and surveyed its smooth white surface unhappily.

"It seems to me," said Elizabeth, "that if they covered up the tunnel entrance that someone must have made a plan for it and kept a record of it. Something so unusual must have been talked about."

"I think so, too," said Cent. "The Navy keeps a record of everything. Someone must know about it."

"Know about what?" said a deep voice.

The girls turned, startled. Captain Ellis was standing by the door.

"Oh, Captain Ellis, we've had such an exciting idea," cried Cent.

"You must tell me about it," said Captain Ellis, looking at his watch. "I have a minute to spare."

"It will take more than a minute," said Elizabeth.

"Perhaps Pacita should tell it," said Cent. "It is about her father."

"Then in that case let's get your father over, Cent. Perhaps I can reach him at his office," said Captain Ellis.

Ten minutes later they were all seated on the porch.

"Now tell us this idea," said Captain Ellis.

"You tell, Cent," said Elizabeth and Pacita.

Cent began at the beginning, retelling the long story Pacita had told them the night before and ending with the exciting idea that the diary might still be in the tunnel. "But where is the tunnel entrance?" she finished.

"Public Works should know," said Commander Hawes. "I'll ask Mr. Gonzales. Perhaps he knows about it. It's an interesting idea, Cent, but not anything to count on."

"We could hardly tear the house down just on the slim hope—" began Captain Ellis.

"Sir," interrupted Elizabeth, looking straight at her stepfather, "if we knew where the entrance was, and I don't see why you can't find out, then it wouldn't be much trouble to get one of those noisy machines to tear up the cement around that one spot."

"I can't go around demolishing the quarters just on a whim. I'm responsible for—" Captain Ellis broke off as Elizabeth jumped up from her chair and glared at him.

"You *can* do it, you know you can," she cried hotly. "All you have to do is say the word. You just don't want to!"

"That's not true!" cried Captain Ellis, jumping up also.

Cent suddenly caught her father's eye, and they both broke into spontaneous laughter.

Captain Ellis and Elizabeth turned to look at them and then rather sheepishly looked at each other again.

"I told you, Elizabeth," said Cent, still laughing, "all you need is a good fight once in a while."

"All right," said Captain Ellis. "We'll find the tunnel, and we'll dig it up."

"Oh, Dad," said Elizabeth, "you're—you're simply *wizard!*"

twenty-four

Mrs. Ellis awakened the girls early the next morning. The workmen would soon be there to begin searching for the opening of the old tunnel entrance.

They ate their breakfast quickly and ran out on the terrace to wait under the beach umbrella. It was drizzling as usual.

In a few minutes a truck drew up to the back of the quarters. Several workmen jumped out and began to unload unusual tools. At the same moment the Captain's car drove into the driveway with Captain Ellis, Commander Hawes, and the public works officer.

Mrs. Ellis and the girls stood in an excited knot as the

workers located the spot on a chart held by the public works officer.

"This is it, sir," said the foreman of the work crew. "According to the chart, this should be the spot. And it taps right," he added, sounding it with an iron bar.

"Then open it up," said Captain Ellis.

The man with the air hammer tightened his goggles, and giving the signal to the man on the truck began the deafening job of cement breaking.

The cement began to crumble slowly under the impact of the machine.

Oh, what a surprise for Dr. O'Dell if we find the book; when we find the book, Cent said to herself. *When* we find the book, she repeated in her mind. We must find it, we must find it, we will find it.

Elizabeth reached over and gave Cent's hand a squeeze. Her fingers were icy cold with excitement. The tense little group of people stood raptly watching as the cement gave way in crumbling lumps.

"It's coming," shouted Captain Ellis, raising his hand in a happy salute to Pacita.

In the middle of the cement a small dark hole began to show. The worker nodded his head and his mouth formed the words, "this is it."

Cent and Elizabeth grabbed Pacita's limp little hands and drew her forward, but they were motioned back by

Captain Ellis. The noise went on interminably, and the dry cement dust continued to fly in such a cloud that the girls could not see the hole.

Finally the worker stepped back, motioned to the helper on the truck, and the shattering racket of the machine stopped.

"Here she is, sir. It's a tunnel all right. First I ever heard of it. I can make the entrance bigger with a hand tool now."

The dust died down and the girls drew forward, breathlessly leaning over to see the black hole that lay below them, a rock-walled tunnel entrance, ancient and mysterious.

"Better stand back, miss," cautioned the foreman. "There might be poison gases in there. First we'll run a ventilator tube in."

"How long will that take?" asked Elizabeth.

"Not long," said the public works officer. "The man who goes down first will wear a mask and take a tank of air, just as a diver does. I think he's about ready to go now."

"Could we go, Dad?" asked Cent.

"Elizabeth may not," said Mrs. Ellis firmly. "Not with her lung injury just healing."

"But couldn't Pacita and I go and help search for the book?" begged Cent.

"We'll see," said Commander Hawes.

"Look," cried Elizabeth. "He's ready to go down."

Cent, Elizabeth, and Pacita crowded in as close as they dared, peering over the edge as the man in the mask began his descent into the mouldy, rocked tunnel.

The entrance was dark and dank. The man flashed his light inside, showing worn old stone stairs leading to the passage below. There was barely room for the man to squeeze through. In a moment he was out of sight.

"I hope he knows what he's looking for," said Cent.

"He does," said Commander Hawes. "Captain Ellis and I told him to examine every crevice in the wall and to lift any loose stones he found and to bring back anything unusual he encountered."

"How long will it take?" asked Cent, nervously ruffling her hair.

"I don't know," said her father.

Elizabeth clasped and unclasped her hands. She bit her underlip, saying nothing.

Pacita kept her eyes focussed on the entrance. "I think," she said, "that the book would surely be near this end. Leon probably just dropped it in, not going in himself, as Father was not with him to guard the entrance."

At this moment the flashlight shone on the steps and the head of the masked man appeared as he climbed back to the surface, carrying only the flashlight in his hands.

"Where is the book? Oh, where is it?" cried Cent.

"He didn't find it," said Pacita, turning away to hide her face.

The explorer pulled off his mask.

"It's no use," he said. "That tunnel is caved in. Must have gotten a direct bomb hit. That must be why they sealed it over. There is no possible way to get through."

"But the book would be near this end anyhow," protested Cent. "Pacita thinks so, and so do I."

"How is the air in there?" asked Commander Hawes.

"It's all right for a quick look according to the instruments," said the man, "but there's nothing in there. I felt every rock."

"But let Pacita and me go look for ourselves; please, Dad," begged Cent.

"All right, I'll go with you. We'll all need flashlights."

"I'll come too," said Captain Ellis.

"I'll go find some extra torches in the house," said Elizabeth. She was back in a moment with flashlights. She handed one to Pacita and Cent.

"Good luck," she whispered. "I think you'll find it."

Captain Ellis went first, inching his way into the narrow passage. He ran his hands over the musty stones, feeling for a break in the masonry. Cent went next, peering anxiously, carefully, at every inch of the steps and the wall.

"Pacita, let's wait until they come out," said Commander Hawes. "Four of us would be too crowded in there."

For five minutes Cent and Captain Ellis flashed their lights, feeling, looking. There was nothing, not even a spider.

"Let's get out now," said Captain Ellis, taking a last look at the pile of dirt and rocks that cut off the rest of the tunnel.

Cent walked back into the light dizzily breathing in the fresh air. She didn't even speak as her father and Pacita went down the steps for their try. Obviously the book was not there. She flopped down in a canvas chair and put her head in her hands.

"A for effort," said Cent as Pacita came up from the tunnel empty handed. "I always thought if you tried hard enough that things would work out." There were tears in her eyes.

Pacita sat down beside her. "Thank you," she said. "I want Father to know how hard you tried."

"Thank you, too, Dad," said Elizabeth, turning to her stepfather. "You did everything you could, for me."

"Shall I fill it up again, sir?" asked the foreman.

"Yes, cover it up," said Captain Ellis. "It was a good idea, but it didn't work."

twenty-five

The rain fell harder as they gathered for lunch. Cent pushed away her dessert. This time she really didn't want it. The telephone rang for Elizabeth. It was Bebe, suggesting that all of them go to the afternoon movie.

They welcomed the idea. It would be good to obliterate their thoughts for a few hours.

"Besides," said Pacita, "I have only seen a few movies in my life. I would like very much to see another one."

In spite of the movie, that day and the next seemed flat indeed. Without speaking of it the whole household was braced for the next dispatch from Washington. The case of Dr. O'Dell would have to be settled one way or another before long.

Mrs. Hawes stopped by to see Cent.

"You look peaked, dear. Would you like to come home again?" she asked.

"Oh no, Mother. I can't now. Elizabeth and I must stay with Pacita now until something is decided."

"Pacita's father may have to stand trial before long. Dad said to tell you that he had talked with Dr. O'Dell. He wants to send her back to the mission in the mountains until everything is settled."

The three girls were out on the terrace the next morning between showers. The gardener was there, cleaning up the mess left by the work crew.

"Good morning, ma'am," said the fellow. "I hear they found the tunnel under the terrace."

"Yes, they did," said Elizabeth. "But nothing came of it."

"I wondered why they opened it. Could I ask you why, miss?"

"You're Jose, aren't you?" asked Cent. "You work on the hill sometimes, don't you?"

"Yes, ma'am. I trim the grass in the park on the hill."

"We were looking for something in the tunnel," said Elizabeth. "We thought it might be there. Had you known of the tunnel before?"

"Not before yesterday," said Jose, leaning on his rake. "The truck crew told me about opening it up, and I told my old father about it last night."

"Had he heard of it?" asked Cent with interest.

"Oh yes, ma'am," said Jose. "He himself had been in the tunnel before it was sealed."

"He went in it?" asked Cent leaning forward.

"He told me last night a strange story about the tunnel."

Pacita stood up and walked over to Jose, her eyes burning.

"Did you hear, did your father hear that a doctor gave drugs to the guerillas by using that tunnel?"

"No, ma'am, I did not hear that. My people were not here in the war. We came here at the end of the war to work. We came from Panay."

"What did your father tell you?" asked Elizabeth.

Jose, surprised at the stir of attention he had created, cleared his throat.

"My father was one of the workmen who helped rebuild this base. He helped lay this terrace. He was here working when they capped the tunnel. He was sitting with the other workmen eating his noontime rice when one of the workers, a curious-minded fellow, went into the tunnel. He wanted to look, to be sure nothing would be sealed up in there. And he found something."

"What? What did he find?" cried all three girls at once.

"He found a small black book written in a strange language. He thought it was Japanese. When the man in charge, a Filipino officer it was, came by the man gave the book to him."

"What happened to it? Where is it?" cried Cent.

"My old father recalls the officer. His name was Captain Aviles. He told my father that the book was not Japanese, but it was in code, and he could not read it. He said he would turn it over to our government to go in a war museum one day."

"Mummy, Mummy," cried Elizabeth. "Oh, Mummy. Get through to Daddy. We've found the black book!"

It took two hours of telephoning to the Philippine Army Headquarters in Manila to locate Captain, now Colonel, Aviles.

"Yes, Captain Ellis," he said when he was finally reached on the wire, "I recall perfectly the black book filled with symbols of a code."

"Where is the book now?" asked Captain Ellis eagerly.

"The book is in the archives of our country. I will check the matter for you, Captain, and report to you later."

Pacita, Elizabeth, and Cent nibbled nervously at their dinner that night, hoping to hear from Colonel Aviles. But it was nearly noon the next day before the word came through. The book had been located in the files and was on its way to Captain Ellis by special messenger.

Pacita raised her eyes to Captain Ellis. "Would you let me take it to my Father myself? Could I, would it be possible?"

"Of course it's possible," said Captain Ellis. "Even the weather is helping today. As soon as the book arrives, which should be within the hour, I will go with you to take it. Perhaps then he will come back with us."

"Please, could Cent and I go too?" asked Elizabeth eagerly.

"No," said her father firmly, "only Pacita and I and the legal officer and Commander Hawes, if he wishes, are going."

"Oh." Elizabeth looked down in dejection.

"Elizabeth," said Cent, grinning a little, "now that you know how to ask your father for things you have to be braced for a 'no' once in a while."

"I don't mind a 'no,' " said Elizabeth, looking up at her father from under her yellow hair which had fallen across her face. "He knows when to say yes, and when to say no. It makes me feel as if I'm not just Mummy's project any more."

"Elizabeth!" said her mother in a shocked tone. "The idea!"

Captain Ellis laughed. "Jenny, don't you know not to come between a father and daughter? You leave us alone."

twenty-six

"I wonder how it will be," said Cent to Elizabeth as they lounged on the porch waiting for Pacita to come back.

"I, too," said Elizabeth. "Pacita was absolutely so excited that it was holy, almost, the way her eyes were shining. It was rather as though she were at the end of a great pilgrimage."

"That's probably the way she felt about it," said Cent.

"I wonder what he will do first," pondered Elizabeth.

"I suppose he'll come back with them, won't he?" said Cent.

"There they come now," cried Elizabeth. The truck was

just then turning into the driveway with Pacita, Dr. O'Dell, Commander Hawes, and the legal officer squeezed in it.

Pacita bounded out, sparkling and chattering.

"Oh," she cried, "oh, oh!" She ran to Elizabeth and Cent and threw her arms around them. "I have everything, my father and friends, such friends."

Dr. O'Dell came behind her. How different he looks, thought Cent, with his face happy.

"Come in, come in, Doctor," said Captain Ellis.

Dr. O'Dell stood a moment looking at the house and the people at the door.

"Excuse me if it takes me a minute to collect myself. I am trying to think how to say thank you to my daughter's friends—to my friends who believed in me." He looked at the girls.

Cent felt such a throbbing in her heart, such a glow of excitement, such hot and cold prickles. She thought, *I'll burst. I'll burst wide open with joy.*

"But I'm the one to say thank you," began Elizabeth, holding out her hand to the doctor.

"Come, come, all this sentiment is too much for me," said Captain Ellis a trifle loudly. "Let's all go in. I'd like to fix you up with some clothes, Doctor, if you like. We're about the same size."

"Thank you, Captain," said Dr. O'Dell, looking down

at his ragged clothes. "I think I could stand a change."

Commander Hawes and the legal officer sat down on the porch with the girls while Mrs. Ellis went to telephone Cent's mother.

"We must all have a big family party here tonight," she announced. "A celebration party."

"Tell us what happened," Cent asked her father when Pacita went inside to clean up for dinner.

"You can easily guess," said Commander Hawes. "Dr. O'Dell took the book unbelievingly at first, and then he lit up with almost a rapture when he saw it all there, his record with dates and names. What will be the legal procedure from now on, Bill?" he asked the legal officer.

"It's relatively simple," replied the lawyer. "The information in the book will make it easy to verify the doctor's story. The guerilla activity is documented now. There will have to be a hearing, of course. Everything can be cleared up simply enough, I believe. And there will be some back pay coming to him, no doubt. His past record will be in his favor, and his humane conduct in the jungle will make his a special case."

"What will Dr. O'Dell do now?" asked Elizabeth. "Do you think he will go back to the United States to live?"

Pacita had slipped back out to the porch. "I don't think he will. He wants me to go there so that I can meet my American relatives and go to school. But he has told me he wants to spend his life here helping the people who have no other doctor."

"Maybe he can build a hospital," said Cent.

"That is my hope," said Dr. O'Dell, coming out the door.

They all looked up, startled, staring in disbelief at the immaculate red-bearded man who stood beside his host. In casual tropical white clothes, he looked impressively handsome.

"I want to go back to America and study again and then come back here. I want to build a memorial clinic to Leon, the Filipino who gave his life for the Americans and his own country."

"Will you build it in the jungle, Dr. O'Dell?" asked Cent.

"No, I would like to build it on the edge of the jungle, halfway between two worlds," he answered.

"Hi, everybody," chirped Jemima, running in the door. She threw herself on Cent. "Oh, I've missed you, Cent, and Mother has made me stay away because she said you were growing up." She drew back and looked at Cent. "I hope it's over now and you're all grown. It's stinking in that room all by myself."

Cent laughed and squeezed Jemima tight. "I missed you, too."

"And let me tell you something else, Cent. I've grown up too. I'm never going to jump on your bed again. It's positively the end."

"The end?" said Mrs. Hawes, coming in the door with a chocolate pie balanced in each hand. "Just a little offering," she explained, handing them to Mrs. Ellis. "What's the end?"

"It's a happy ending, that's what," said Cent.

"So it is," said Elizabeth.

"And a happy beginning too," added Pacita.

About the Author

Cora Cheney, who is Mrs. Benjamin W. Partridge, Jr. in private life, is the mother of four children ranging from a nine-year-old girl to a college-age boy. It is a peripatetic family, for Benjamin Partridge is Captain B. W. Partridge, Jr. of the United States Navy, and he and his family have been stationed all over the world. In seven years they have visited twenty-six different countries—from Rhode Island to the Philippines, from France to, at this point, Iceland and back to Rhode Island.

Wherever they are stationed, however, Cora Cheney has been writing. Her books, which often have exotic settings that reflect her current home, are suspense-filled and popular with young readers. THE DOLL OF LILAC VALLEY, THE GIRL AT JUNGLE'S EDGE, and THE PEG LEGGED PIRATE OF SULU are some of her Borzoi Books.

A NOTE ON THE TYPE

This book is set in Granjon, a type named in compliment to ROBERT GRANJON, *but neither a copy of a classic face nor an entirely original creation. George W. Jones drew the basic design for this type from classic sources, but deviated from his model to profit by the intervening centuries of experience and progress. This type is based primarily upon the type used by Claude Garamond (1510–61) in his beautiful French books, and more closely resembles Garamond's own than do any of the various modern types that bear his name.*

Of Robert Granjon nothing is known before 1545, except that he had begun his career as type-cutter in 1523. The boldest and most original designer of his time, he was one of the first to practise the trade of type-founder apart from that of printer. Between 1549 and 1551 he printed a number of books in Paris, also continuing as type-cutter. By 1557 he was settled in Lyons and had married Antoinette Salamon, whose father, Bernard, was an artist associated with Jean de Tournes. Between 1557 and 1562 Granjon printed about twenty books in types designed by himself, following, after the fashion of the day, the cursive handwriting of the time. These types, usually known as caractères de civilité, *he himself called* lettres françaises, *as especially appropriate to his own country. He was granted a monopoly of these types for ten years, but they were soon copied. Granjon appears to have lived in Antwerp for a time, but was at Lyons in 1575 and 1577, and for the next decade at Rome, working for the Vatican and Medici presses, his work consisting largely in cutting exotic types. Towards the end of his life he may have returned to live in Paris, where he died in 1590.*